DELTORA QUEST 3

The Sister of the South

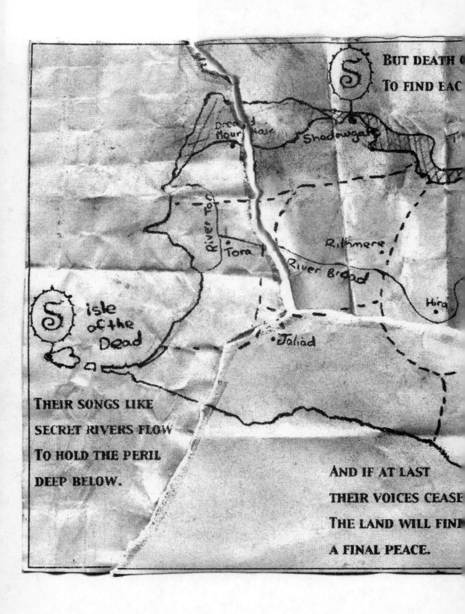

BUT DEATH O[...]

TO FIND EAC[...]

Dread
Mountain

Shadowgat[...]

River Tor

Tora

Rithmere

River Broad

Hira[...]

Isle
of the
Dead

Jaliad

THEIR SONGS LIKE
SECRET RIVERS FLOW
TO HOLD THE PERIL
DEEP BELOW.

AND IF AT LAST
THEIR VOICES CEASE
THE LAND WILL FIN[...]
A FINAL PEACE.

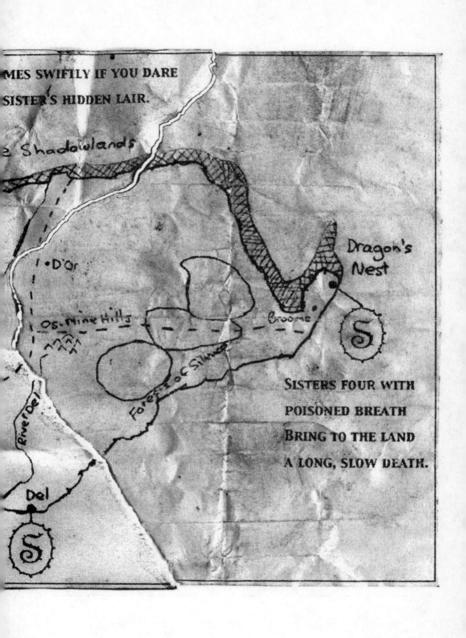

MES SWIFTLY IF YOU DARE

SISTER'S HIDDEN LAIR.

e Shadowlands

• D'Or

Os-Mine Hills

River Del

Forests of Silence

Broome

Dragon's Nest

S

SISTERS FOUR WITH
POISONED BREATH
BRING TO THE LAND
A LONG, SLOW DEATH.

Del

S

DELTORA QUEST 3

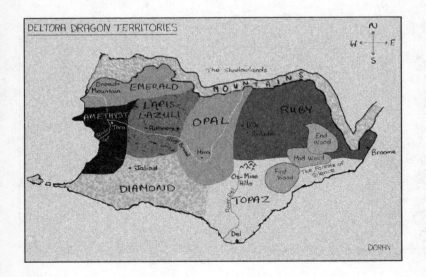

DELTORA QUEST 3

The Sister of the South

Emily Rodda

A Scholastic Press book
from
Scholastic Australia

For Reuben Jakeman

LEXILE™ 830

Scholastic Press
345 Pacific Highway
Lindfield NSW 2070
An imprint of Scholastic Australia Pty Limited (ABN 11 000 614 577)
PO Box 579
Gosford NSW 2250
www.scholastic.com.au

Part of the Scholastic Group
Sydney ● Auckland ● New York ● Toronto ● London ● Mexico City
● New Delhi ● Hong Kong ● Buenos Aires ● Puerto Rico

First published by Scholastic Australia in 2004.
Text and graphics copyright © Emily Rodda, 2004.
Graphics by Kate Rowe.
Cover illustrations copyright © Scholastic Australia, 2004.
Cover illustrations by Marc McBride.

National Library of Australia Cataloguing-in-Publication entry
    Rodda, Emily, 1948- .
    The sister of the south.
    For children aged 9 years and over.
    ISBN 1 86504 616 7.
    I. Title. (Series : Rodda, Emily, 1948- Deltora quest 3 ; 4).
A823.3

Typeset in Palatino.

Printed by McPherson's Printing Group, Victoria.

10 9 8 7 6 5 4 3 2 1   4 5 6 7 8 / 0

CONTENTS

The story so far . . .

Lief, Barda and Jasmine are on a quest to find and destroy the Four Sisters, evil Shadow Lord creations which have been poisoning Deltora for centuries. They learned of the Four Sisters plot through the Enemy's crystal, left in the palace in Del after the Belt of Deltora was restored and the Shadow Lord's tyranny over Deltora ended.

To succeed in his quest, Lief must wake Deltora's last dragons from their enchanted sleep, for only when the power of a dragon joins the power of a gem in the magic Belt of Deltora can a Sister be destroyed.

Centuries ago, Deltora's dragons, fierce protectors of their land, were hunted almost to extinction by the Enemy's seven Ak-Baba. When only one dragon from each gem territory remained, the explorer Doran the Dragonlover persuaded the beasts to sleep in safety until a king, wearing the Belt of Deltora, called them to wake.

Too late, Doran learned of the Shadow Lord's plan to use the Four Sisters to starve Deltora's people. Now that the dragons had gone, there was nothing to stop the Enemy from putting the Sisters into place. Doran tried to warn of the danger, but was not believed. Leaving a map showing where he thought the Sisters were, he set out to find proof. But the Enemy wreaked a hideous revenge upon him on the Isle of the Dead, and his map was torn into four parts, and hidden.

Despite terrible dangers, Lief, Barda and Jasmine have managed to find all the fragments of Doran's map, and to destroy the Sisters of the East, North and West. They have also found Red Han, the lost keeper of the magic Bone Point lighthouse, raising hopes that trading ships loaded with badly-needed food may now sail to Deltora across the western seas.

But the companions cannot rest. To their amazement and horror, the final map fragment has shown that the last Sister, the Sister of the South, is in their home city of Del. This is very bad news. Jasmine's father, the legendary Resistance leader, Doom, is already struggling to prevent Del's starving people from sinking into despair. Lief's mother, Sharn, who might bring the people comfort, is still in Tora, Del's magic sister city in the west. Messages from Josef, the old palace librarian, are increasingly confused and frantic. And wherever they are, whatever they do, it seems the Shadow Lord's eyes are upon them.

Now read on . . .

1 - Bad Tidings

The grave of Doran the Dragonlover contained only his silver flask and a strange, gleaming many-coloured stone. These ancient objects were all that remained of Deltora's greatest explorer.

The grave was in as wild a place as Doran could have wished—looking over the windswept rock that pointed to the Isle of the Dead, where the Sister of the West had been destroyed.

Lief, Barda and Jasmine stood at the graveside. With them were Ava the fortune-teller and Red Han, the lost keeper of the Bone Point Light. There were also two dragons—Veritas, dragon of the amethyst, and the orphaned baby dragon of the diamond, who was as yet unnamed. And it was these two, Lief thought, whose presence would have pleased Doran the most.

After careful thought, Veritas had scratched the lettering upon the grave marker.

'It is fitting that we used his true name,' Veritas said quietly. 'For dragons, to know a true name is to have power over that name's owner. But Dragonfriend is at peace. Nothing can harm him now.'

As Lief turned away from the grave, his heart was very full. He knew that the many-coloured stone was Doran's soul-stone, filled with the great explorer's memories. When Lief had placed it in its final resting place, his mind had been flooded with pictures.

Wild and beautiful places. Thousands of faces. The secret seas of the underworld. Flying with dragons . . .

And through it all ran Doran's voice, whispering in a strange language. Whispering, it seemed, of Veritas.

Veritas hopian forta fortuna fidelis honora joyeu . . .
Veritas hopian forta fortuna fidelis honora joyeu . . .

No doubt Veritas would know what the words meant, but Lief could not ask. The soul-stone had shown him the secrets of Doran's heart. He felt he had no right to speak of them.

'You were always in Doran's mind, I think,' he

contented himself with saying to the grieving dragon, when it, too, turned from the grave.

'As he will always be in mine,' said Veritas. 'That is why, though I long to return to my own territory, I will stay here for a time. The diamond infant must be taught to know her own land, and the ways of dragons. Dragonfriend would have wished it.'

An hour later, the companions set off along the broad coast road, with Red Han striding eagerly before them, and their horses, Honey, Bella and Swift, trotting no less eagerly behind.

Kree had left hours earlier, carrying a message for Zeean that all was well, that Red Han had been found, and that the companions, and the lighthouse keeper, wished to be sped to Tora.

Plainly the message had been safely delivered, for already the travellers could feel the faint tug of Toran magic. By nightfall they would be in the white city of the west.

There, Red Han would find the help he needed to return to Bone Point, where he longed to be. And there Lief, Barda and Jasmine and the horses would find food, rest, and then safe, quick passage to Del, their final goal.

'How I long for a hot bath and a comfortable bed!' Barda exclaimed.

'It is fresh fruit I long for,' sighed Jasmine, and Filli, riding on her shoulder, chattered fervent agreement.

The magic strengthened, and they began to move

faster. Crisp, salty wind beat against their faces. They exclaimed and pointed at the sea birds swooping over the waves close to shore, feasting on the tiny fish that swarmed just below the sparkling surface.

Only twenty-four hours had passed since the destruction of the Sister of the West, but already the land and sea were coming to life.

So it will be in Del, Lief thought. So it will be in the whole of the south, if we can find the last Sister.

Plainly Jasmine's thoughts had been running along the same lines.

'I cannot think where the Sister of the South might be hidden in a bustling place like Del,' she said. 'Could it be buried deep on the shore, perhaps?'

'It is hard to imagine it,' Barda frowned. 'At the time the Sister was hidden, Del harbour was a busy port—always crowded with boats and people.'

'I was thinking of the maze of drain tunnels beneath the city,' Lief said.

'Of course!' Barda's face lit up. 'One of those tunnels begins in the palace. Doom knows of it—has even used it. It would have been simple for the Shadow Lord servant Drumm, the king's chief advisor in those days, to creep out through that tunnel and put the Sister somewhere in the maze.'

'And easy for him, and all the chief advisors who followed him, to visit it in secret, and protect it,' Lief added.

'But there are no longer chief advisors in the palace,'

Jasmine put in. 'Who protects the Sister now?'

'Indeed,' Barda said heavily. 'Who is the new guardian? It could be anyone. Del is a large place.'

'It is,' Lief said. 'But very few people in it have any way of finding out where we are or what we are doing. Yet time and again the Shadow Lord has known where to find us.'

'That may have nothing to do with the guardian of the south,' Barda said. 'I have begun to wonder whether something we are carrying helps the Enemy track us. I suggest we leave our packs—even our garments— behind us when we depart for Del.'

Lief nodded agreement. He was remembering Ava's voice hissing in his ear as he bid her farewell.

'Beware, Lief of Del!' the blind fortune-teller had whispered. 'You might have faced the Kobb of the Isle of the Dead and survived, but I see creeping darkness in your future. The way upon which you have set your feet leads to disaster. Heed my warning, and turn aside from it!'

'I cannot do that, Ava,' Lief had said gently.

And Ava had stumped away from him in anger, muttering and hunching her shoulders.

Jasmine's voice broke into Lief's thoughts. 'We have almost reached the border,' she cried. 'Soon we will be caught in the magic of Tora, and we will fly!'

In Tora, a great crowd was waiting to greet them. The horses were led away to be cared for. Red Han was escorted to the feast that had been prepared. And soon Lief, Barda and Jasmine were alone in the great marble square with only Zeean, Marilen, Ranesh and Manus the Ralad man.

Surprised, Lief looked around for his mother.

'Sharn returned to Del,' Zeean said quietly. 'It seems that the city is being besieged by a golden dragon. The people are arming themselves, and demanding that the dragon be hunted down.'

'No!' Lief exclaimed in horror. 'The dragon of the topaz must not be harmed!'

'Sharn seemed to know that,' said Manus, his black eyes grave. 'She believed she could calm the people. She left for Del the moment she heard the news—the same day we heard that you were safe in the Sleeping Dunes. But—'

'But what?' Lief cried, in a fever of impatience.

'You must prepare yourself for a shock, Lief,' Zeean said bluntly. 'Almost as soon as she arrived at the palace, Sharn fell ill. And I fear it is no ordinary illness. It is a deadly infection, now spreading very fast through the city. Your mother still lives, but hundreds of others in Del have died.'

Lief stared, aghast. Jasmine put her arm around him.

'Does not the diamond in the Belt of Deltora protect from pestilence?' she said. 'And it gives strength, as well. Never fear, Lief. Sharn will recover as soon as you reach her, I am sure of it.'

6

'What is this illness?' Barda demanded. 'Does it have a name?'

Zeean's lips tightened. 'It has been *given* a name,' she said curtly. 'Because Sharn was the first to fall ill, your people appear to believe that she was the one who carried the disease to Del. They are calling it the Toran Plague.'

She thrust two notes into Lief's hands. 'The bird Ebony brought the one from Doom an hour ago,' she said. 'The other came on the day Sharn left us.'

'It is from Josef, by the hand,' Ranesh muttered. 'He is becoming more and more desperate. I should go to him, but—'

'But your place is with your wife, who is with child, and needs you,' Zeean broke in. 'Josef has more than enough people to tend to him.'

She turned to Lief, Barda and Jasmine. 'Manus and I must go,' she said. 'Red Han wishes to go to Bone Point at once, so the Light can shine this very night. Food awaits you in the dining hall, and your chambers have been prepared. Rest well.'

She swept away, her back very straight, with Manus trotting after her.

'Zeean grieves for Sharn. And it hurts her that Tora is being blamed for the plague,' Marilen said in her soft voice.

'Ah yes,' said Ranesh drily. 'For, of course, only good can come from Tora.'

Marilen glanced at him. 'Let us go and fetch food

from the dining hall,' she murmured. 'Our friends will prefer to eat in a quiet place, I am sure.'

The moment Marilen and Ranesh were gone, Lief opened Doom's note.

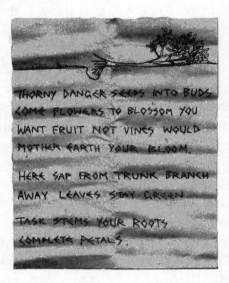

THORNY DANGER SEEPS INTO BUDS
COME FLOWERS TO BLOSSOM YOU
WANT FRUIT NOT VINES WOULD
MOTHER EARTH YOUR BLOOM.

HERE SAP FROM TRUNK BRANCH
AWAY LEAVES STAY GREEN

TASK STEMS YOUR ROOTS
COMPLETE PETALS.

Slowly, following the code, Lief read out each sentence backwards, leaving out all words that had anything to do with plants.

'"Your mother would not want you to come into danger. Stay away from here. Complete your task."'

Barda gave a mirthless laugh. 'To complete our task, we *must* go to Del. But, of course, Doom does not know that.'

Slowly Lief opened the second, older note—the note from Josef.

> Lief—I seize this chance to write again—must beg your pardon for troubling you. I long to talk to you—see you—you have much to do, however—urgent matters to attend to. Forgive me—fearful old Josef—news of you will come soon no doubt. Keep well—tell your companions the same—no one misses you all more than I do.
>
> Josef
>
>
> P.S. So many dashes! They show my state of mind. I pray you will understand. The message, after all, comes from my heart.

Frowning, Lief passed the paper to Barda and Jasmine.

'His mind is failing, I fear,' Barda said, after a moment.

Lief sighed. It seemed that Barda was right. And yet . . .

'Someone has read this before us!' Jasmine exclaimed, tapping the note. 'Look! There are two sets of fold lines on the paper. It has been opened, then folded again in haste.'

'That is no mystery,' said Barda. 'I have no doubt that Doom reads every note sent from the palace, in case it might be helpful to a spy.'

'Then he wasted his time with this,' Jasmine said, handing the letter back to Lief. 'It says nothing at all.'

Lief read the note again. He could not rid himself of the feeling that there was something strange about it. The words seemed hasty and confused. Yet the old librarian's handwriting was just as usual.

He glanced at the lines below the signature.

So many dashes! . . . I pray you will understand. The message, after all, comes from my heart . . .

Lief's skin prickled.

. . . dashes . . . the message, after all . . .

Lief went back to the beginning of the note, but this time he read only those words that came after a dash.

—I . . . —must . . . —see . . . —you . . . —urgent . . . —fearful . . . —news . . . —tell . . . —no-one.

I must see you. Urgent. Fearful news. Tell no-one.

2 - The Dream

L ief felt the blood rush into his face. What news was so fearful that even Jasmine and Barda were not to know of it? Or Doom? For plainly Josef had written his message in code so it would escape Doom's notice.

The news could not be about the plague, or about Sharn's illness. The letter had been written before either of those things had happened.

Possibly Josef's mind really *was* failing and his 'fearful news' was just some foolish fancy. But what if it was not? What if he had discovered where the Sister of the South was hidden?

'Does any of the Kin's Dreaming Water remain, Jasmine?' Lief asked abruptly.

'A little,' Jasmine said. 'It should be enough for you to see Sharn.' She pulled a small flask from one of her pockets and held it out.

Lief took the flask with a muttered word of thanks. He disliked allowing his friends to believe he wished to see his mother, when in fact he wanted the Dreaming Water for something else. But he had no choice. He had to keep faith with Josef—at least until he had seen how things were, and had made up his mind what to do.

Later, alone in his cool, white Toran bed chamber, Lief drained the flask of Dreaming Water, and thought of Josef. He crawled into bed and lay still, but his mind was too active for rest. It seemed hours before exhaustion finally overcame him and he slept.

Almost at once, he began to dream.

He found himself standing just inside Josef's room at the back of the library. Josef was hunched over his desk, his back to the door, working by the light of a candle. To his left was a stack of paper neatly tied with blue ribbon. To his right lay an open volume of the *Deltora Annals* and a clutter of paint pots, brushes, pens and empty tea cups. His body hid whatever was directly in front of him.

Lief's heart began to thud as he moved further into the room. He found himself treading softly, though he knew he could not be heard or seen. With every step, he became more shocked and grieved. Even from behind, it was easy to see that Josef was sadly changed.

The old librarian's white hair was dull, and much of it had fallen out so that patches of pink scalp showed between the long strands. The warm rug draped around his shoulders could not disguise how frail he was.

As Lief watched, Josef pushed aside a metal ruler with which he had been working. The hand clutching the ruler was like a blue-veined claw.

But Josef was not like this when we left Del! Lief thought in dismay. How could he have weakened so quickly?

He jumped as Josef groaned.

'No, there is no doubt,' the old man mumbled. 'I have made no mistake. Oh, what wicked trickery is this? If only I had seen it before! If only I had remembered! Fool! Fool!'

Lief moved closer. He was just about to peer over Josef's shoulder when there was the sound of loud footsteps outside in the library.

Josef started violently. His bony hand shot out and grasped the open volume of the *Deltora Annals*. Paint pots and cups overturned as he dragged the book to the centre of the desk, covering whatever lay there.

Doom strode into the room, dragging Josef's assistant, Paff, by the back of her collar. He was scowling ferociously. Paff's eyes were bulging with fright.

Josef turned to face them. His face was gaunt, his eyes were dark hollows. But still he straightened his shoulders and climbed to his feet, making a pathetic attempt to appear in control of the situation.

'What is the meaning of this?' he quavered.

'Lindal of Broome caught your assistant trying to creep into Sharn's room, Josef,' Doom said coldly. He shook Paff like a puppy, and a choking sob burst from her lips.

Josef's hand tightened on the back of the chair. 'Release her, if you please,' he said in a high voice. 'She was only doing my bidding.'

Doom's eyes seemed to flash. 'So it seems,' he said. 'She was carrying this.'

He held a paper out in front of him. Lief read it, his heart sinking.

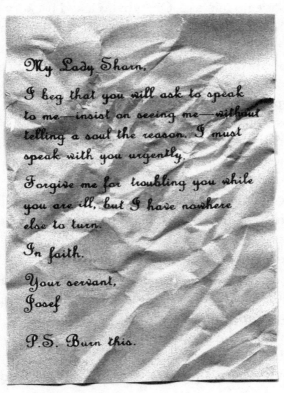

My Lady Sharn,

I beg that you will ask to speak to me—insist on seeing me—without telling a soul the reason. I must speak with you urgently.

Forgive me for troubling you while you are ill, but I have nowhere else to turn.

In faith.

Your servant,

Josef

P.S. Burn this.

'Did I not tell you, Josef, that Sharn is gravely ill?' Doom said through tight lips. 'And did I not tell you that the Toran Plague is highly infectious? By the heavens, can you not smell the funeral fires of those wretched souls who came in contact with her before her illness was known?'

Lief felt cold with dread.

Josef lifted his chin. 'I must see the lady Sharn,' he said stubbornly. 'You have no right to keep me from her, Doom. If Lief were here—'

'Lief is *not* here!' snapped Doom. '*I* am. You cannot see Sharn, Josef. If you have something of importance to say, you can say it to me.'

Josef pressed his lips together and did not speak.

Doom made a disgusted noise, and released his grip on Paff's collar. She darted away from him and scurried to Josef's side.

Together the frail old man and the fluffy-haired girl faced Doom—strange allies in a very unequal battle.

'Keep your secrets, then, Josef!' Doom said angrily. 'But I warn you, the next time you feel like sending Paff on such a mission, think again. She was panting so loudly with fear as she crept up the hallway to Sharn's bed chamber that Lindal heard her through the door!'

Josef glanced at Paff irritably. She flushed pink, and her lips quivered.

'I am sorry, Josef,' she whispered. 'I waited, just as you said, until Lindal of Broome went out for more hot water. She was carrying a jug. I heard her footsteps going

15

away. But it was all a trick! She must have crept back. I had taken but one step into the room when she was upon me!'

Her eyes filled with tears. 'She twisted my arm— treated me like a criminal,' she whispered. 'I am so ashamed.'

'Josef is the one who should be ashamed!' barked Doom. 'Let him do his own dirty work in future!'

Paff looked up. Suddenly her tear-filled eyes were angry.

'Josef can hardly walk!' she cried. 'He cannot go up to Sharn's bed chamber without guards to carry him, you know that! How *can* you taunt him with his weakness!'

'I did not mean—' Doom began impatiently. But now that Paff had begun speaking, it seemed she could not stop.

'And in any case, Josef did not *force* me to help him,' she said. 'I agreed gladly. His old assistant, Ranesh, would have done it in a moment. And I—I am sick to death of being compared to Ranesh and found wanting. I was not going to refuse my one chance to prove myself!'

'I daresay Josef knew that only too well,' said Doom drily.

Lief saw a flicker of shame cross Josef's haggard face, and groaned inwardly.

'Josef, I can waste no more time with you,' Doom said to the old librarian. 'You must cease your troublemaking. You must accept once and for all that

16

you cannot see Sharn.'

'But why should he not see her?' shrilled Paff. 'Why should Lindal of Broome, who is almost a stranger here, sit with the lady Sharn, while Josef is kept away? Is it because Lindal is your ally in all things, and Josef is not?'

Doom's scarred face darkened. His eyes narrowed.

'Paff, go to your room,' Josef muttered urgently.

Red-faced and silent, Paff left his side, edged past Doom and disappeared through the open doorway into the darkness beyond.

Josef watched her go, swaying slightly where he stood.

'I have given you all the news I have, Josef,' Doom hissed. 'Sharn could tell you no more, even if she could speak. I showed you the message from Zeean saying that Lief, Barda and Jasmine had succeeded in the west. Can you not be satisfied with that, and be at peace?'

Josef put a trembling hand to his brow, but said nothing.

'You are not well,' Doom went on in a level voice. 'Your mind is clouded. That girl Paff is too weak-headed to see it, but I see it. And you yourself must know it.'

He looked keenly at the swaying figure before him, and shook his head as if to clear it.

'If I have been impatient with you, Josef, I beg your pardon,' he added. 'But I have not slept more than an hour or two at a time in more days than I can count. And even at the best of times, soft words are not my way.'

For Doom, this was a generous apology. Lief willed Josef to understand. But the old man kept stubborn silence. He stood gripping the back of the chair, his knuckles white, his gaunt face as rigid as a piece of gnarled wood.

Doom cursed under his breath and left the room.

Only when the sound of his footsteps had died away did Josef move. His face sagged with exhaustion. Trembling, he lowered himself into his chair.

'Oh, why does Lief not come?' he whispered. 'Lief must speak to me—he *must*—before anyone else knows he is here—before anything else is done! Did I make that plain enough? I cannot . . . remember.'

Again he put his hand to his brow. 'I *did* send the message, did I not?' he mumbled. 'It was not just a dream? Oh . . . why can I not *think*?'

He buried his face in his hands.

'Josef!' Lief exclaimed in frustration. 'What do you want to tell me? Say it aloud!'

The old man's head jerked up. Slowly he turned in his chair. But the next moment his face had vanished, and Lief was back in bed, blinking up at a white ceiling flooded with moonlight.

He lay still for a moment, gathering his thoughts. Then he jumped out of bed and made for the door.

He regretted having to wake Barda and Jasmine from the first peaceful sleep they had enjoyed in many days. But he could not leave them behind, and they would think his feeling of urgency had been caused by a dream of his mother, and ask no questions.

He had to see Josef. And he could not wait.

In less than an hour, three shadows were speeding towards Del. Only the birds and beasts of the night saw them pass. A few villagers, stirring in their beds, thought they heard the beat of flying hoofs. But the sound passed so quickly that they told themselves they had been dreaming.

Following Barda's plan, Lief, Barda and Jasmine were wearing Toran garments and carrying only their weapons. Their bright robes fluttering in the wind, they bent forward over their horses' necks, lost in a dream of speed.

Back in the white city of the west, Zeean alone was awake. But her will was enough to speed them along the well-worn path to Del.

Kree was flying far behind the horses. The old wound at the back of his neck still troubled him, but he had refused to ride tamely with Filli in the crook of Jasmine's arm. Perhaps he had once or twice allowed himself to be carried on the back of a dragon. But, sped by Toran magic or not, Honey, Bella and Swift were ordinary horses of Del, and Kree was far too proud to ride with them.

He knew Jasmine and Filli were safe, wrapped in Toran magic. So he flew alone beneath the slowly sinking moon, enjoying the night and the silence, taking his time.

Neither he, nor the riders ahead of him, sensed the

moment when an evil presence stirred and woke to knowledge of them. None of them felt the explosion of hatred that erupted at the warning of their approach.

They sped, untroubled, through the night as a liquid black shadow filled with malice slipped beneath a door and began its secret, oozing progress through the darkened palace of Del.

3 - Del

The moon had set and the sun had not yet risen when the companions reached the city gates. The four guards on watch held up their lanterns, saw the horses and the Toran robes of their riders, and drew back, quickly pulling scarfs over their mouths and noses.

'What is your business here, people of Tora?' one of the guards called. He sounded far from friendly.

'We are here to advise Doom on the matter of the Toran Plague,' Jasmine called back, as planned. 'Our presence was requested.'

'We were told of no such request!' snapped the guard.

Jasmine pulled a paper from her pocket. 'I have the message here,' she said. 'Do you wish to see it?'

She urged Swift forward, holding out the paper.

'Halt! Come no closer!' the guard bellowed, taking a hurried step back and pulling his scarf more tightly around his face. 'You may pass. But be aware that if you do, you cannot leave the city again until it is declared free of plague.'

'We understand,' Jasmine said.

'So they will die here, trapped like rats, with the rest of us,' Lief heard one of the other guards growl to his neighbour. 'There is some justice in that, at least.'

The gates swung open. The guards shrank back as far as they could, and waited till the visitors were well past before venturing out of the shadows to close the gates again.

'Disgraceful!' fumed Barda under his breath. 'They did not even *look* at the paper!'

Jasmine shrugged. 'It is fortunate they did not, since it was only a note from Marilen to Sharn, and they would certainly have recognised us if they had looked at us closely.'

Barda scowled. He knew that what she said was true, but his pride in his well-trained guards had been sorely shaken.

'Do not be too hard on them,' said Lief in a low voice. 'They would have faced an enemy without flinching, but disease is fearful to them. It troubles me more that they greeted us with such suspicion—even anger.'

And as he spoke, Jasmine drew breath sharply. She had pulled Swift to a halt, and was staring at a yellow notice stuck to a wall beside her.

'Look at this!' she breathed.

THE TRUTH OF THE TORAN PLAGUE
PEOPLE OF DEL, AWAKE! DO NOT BE DECEIVED!
THE PLAGUE IS NOT A THING OF NATURE. IT HAS BEEN SENT BY TORA TO DESTROY US!
FOR PROOF, READ ON & FACE THE TRUTH.

#TRUTH! The sorcerers of Tora feast & take their ease while all around them work & starve. Yet they demand our goodwill.

#TRUTH! Torans envy Del, because Del is home to Deltora's ruling family. This forced our beloved Lady Sharn to leave us & dwell for months in Tora as hostage to Toran pride.

#TRUTH! Tora's treachery is proved by history. When the Shadow Lord invaded, Tora broke its oath of loyalty and allowed the Enemy to enslave us.

#TRUTH! King Lief, in the innocence & generosity of his youth, forgave the Torans for their treachery & allowed them to return to their enchanted city.

#TRUTH! Tora has repaid the king's trust by plotting to destroy Del by stealth. The Toran plague proves it!

'All its "truths" are lies!' Jasmine exclaimed.

'There is enough truth in most of them to deceive frightened people,' Barda answered grimly. 'There *is* food in Tora. Sharn *did* go there partly to assure the Torans that their friendship was valued. The Torans *did* once break their oath of loyalty, and Lief *did* forgive them—'

'"In the innocence and generosity of his youth",' Lief quoted bitterly. 'The writer might as well have said "his ignorance and foolishness", for that is what is meant.'

He shook his head. 'This notice is so *stupid*! It says it is going to prove that the Torans sent the plague to destroy Del. Then it says that the plague *itself* proves that the Torans are plotting to destroy Del. Where is the logic in that?'

'There is none,' said Barda, ripping the notice from the wall. 'But those looking for someone to blame for their misfortune will not see that, I fear. We had better move on. The sun will soon be rising. If we are seen in the streets wearing Toran garments we could be attacked before we are recognised.'

They rode on, growing more and more uneasy. The air was hazy with the smoke of funeral fires. Fear and strangeness haunted the familiar streets. Now and again they came upon another copy of the hateful yellow notice, stuck to a fence or pole. Plainly the city was full of them.

As they drew nearer to the palace, many of the doors they passed were hung with charms that the owners hoped would protect their homes from illness. An increasing number were nailed shut and marked with a red X to show that the people who had lived there had died of the plague.

At last they reached the bottom of the palace hill. The palace loomed above them. Lief could not see the guards standing by the entrance doors, but he knew they must be there, as they were every night.

It is almost time to make my move, he thought. But before he could speak, Jasmine pulled Swift to a halt once more.

'I will wait here for Kree,' she announced. 'He must not enter the palace alone. The last time he was there, he was poisoned.'

'He slept through a night and a day, and believed he had been drugged,' said Barda. 'But he may have been merely exhausted. Who can say?'

'I will wait,' Jasmine said firmly. 'You and Lief go on.'

'No,' Lief said, swinging down to the ground and thrusting Honey's reins into Jasmine's hands. 'You two wait here for Kree. I will meet you inside.'

And ignoring his companions' startled, furious whispers, he darted off the road and almost at once was swallowed by the darkness.

Toran robes were more suited to strolling along marble pathways than to toiling up a rough hill in the dark. But at last Lief reached his goal—the huge rock in the shape of a sleeping bear that marked the secret way into the palace.

Memories flashed into his mind as he pulled away the grass that masked the tunnel entrance.

The last time he had done this, desperate fear had been driving him. The last time he had done this, the Shadow Lord ruled in Deltora, and Doom, Jasmine and Barda were prisoners, about to be condemned to death.

That time is long gone, he told himself, as he wormed his way into the narrow stone passage. It is foolish, no doubt, for me to be creeping into the palace like a thief. I have been infected by Josef's fancies.

But fear grew in him as he crawled through the black silence of the tunnel. And he did not know if the fear was remembered, or real.

By the time he emerged in the palace chapel, his teeth were chattering. He replaced the floor tile that had sealed the tunnel, wincing at the small, grating sound it made as it slid into place.

Close beside him was the high marble platform that dominated the small room. Lief brushed against it as he stood up, and twitched aside instinctively.

For centuries, the honoured dead of the palace had lain in state on that platform. Lief's own father had rested there for a full day after he died, and Lief had kneeled with his mother in the chill silence of the chapel for a long, sad hour or two. The ritual had brought him no comfort, and he had never visited the chapel since.

Trying to shrug off the feeling of dread that seemed to hang upon him like a heavy cloak, Lief felt his way to the door. Opening it cautiously, he climbed the steps that led up to the huge, echoing space of the entrance hall.

All was silent, but he knew it would not be silent

for long. Kree must have joined Jasmine and Barda by now. Soon his companions would reach the palace. There was no time to waste.

He ran lightly past the stairs and on to the library. He let himself in, and moved quietly through the dimness. Dark shelves towered around him. The familiar smell of old books filled his nose. At the end of the long room, feeble light glimmered through Josef's half-open door.

Lief moved quickly towards the light. When he had almost reached it, he saw another splinter of light to his right, at floor level.

He remembered that Paff also slept in the library, her bed chamber separated from Josef's by a storeroom and the tiny kitchen where she and Josef could heat soup and make tea. Paff's door was closed, but it seemed that she, too, was awake.

Silently, Lief slipped into Josef's room. Josef was slumped over his desk, his head pillowed on his arms. In front of him the candle flickered in a pool of melted wax.

He has fallen asleep over his work, Lief thought. He approached the desk and put a hand on the old man's shoulder.

'Josef,' he whispered. 'It is I, Lief.'

'Lief . . .' The voice was slurred, and very faint. Josef's eyelids fluttered open, but he did not move.

Lief's heart gave a great thud. His grip on Josef's shoulder tightened.

'Lief?' the old man murmured. 'Or . . . another vision?'

'No!' Lief whispered, falling to his knees by the chair. 'No, Josef, this time I am truly here!'

The old librarian blinked. 'Keep away,' he slurred. 'Lief . . . Keep away!'

With an enormous effort, he raised his head. Lief caught his breath as he saw the familiar, wrinkled face gleaming with sweat and hideously disfigured with swollen scarlet blotches.

'The Toran Plague,' Josef murmured. 'Ah, I . . . did not dream there was real danger. Never . . . would I have sent the girl to Sharn if I had known.'

His glazed eyes focused on Lief and flamed with sudden panic.

'Cover your face!' he groaned. 'Get out of this room! Ah, Lief, I beg you! Do not make me a murderer twice over!'

Lief scrambled up and backed away, aghast. 'I—I will fetch help!' he stammered.

'No time,' Josef mumbled. 'I must warn you. The Four Sisters. You . . . the sorcerer . . . you must stop . . .'

'I will, Josef!' Lief said, tears burning at the back of his eyes. 'Three of the four are destroyed already. Do you know where the last is? Is that why you summoned me?'

'Plot,' the old man breathed. 'Treachery. North . . . to south, east . . . to west . . . lines . . . map . . .'

His head drooped as though his neck was too weak

to support it. 'Danger,' he whispered. 'Fearful . . . Must warn—Lief.'

'I am here, Josef,' Lief cried. 'I know that the Sister of the South is in Del. But *where* in Del? Where—?'

Josef's dry lips writhed as he struggled to speak. Lief strained to hear. His ears caught a single word. His eyes widened in disbelief. Could Josef possibly have said 'Here'?

'"Here", Josef?' he gasped. 'In the *palace*?'

The crease between Josef's brows deepened. 'Beware, Lief . . . evil . . . the centre . . . the heart . . . the city . . . of . . .'

The sighing voice trailed away.

Lief turned and ran to Paff's room. He knocked frantically, calling Paff's name, but there was no answer. With a feeling of dread, he tried the door. As he had expected, it was locked.

Lief drew back and kicked. The door shuddered, but held. He gripped the diamond in the Belt and kicked again. The lock burst, and the door swung open.

Paff sat in her bed, propped up on two pillows. She was wearing a long-sleeved pink nightgown. Her yellow hair was neatly braided into two skimpy tails. A book lay open on her lap and the stub of a candle burned low on the bedside table beside a half-drunk cup of tea.

At first glance it looked as if she had simply fallen asleep while reading. But Lief knew this was not so. Paff's head lolled backwards. Her face was shining with sweat. Her limbs were as rigid as if they had been carved out of stone. Saliva dribbled from one corner of her open mouth. Beneath her fluttering eyelids, the whites of her eyes gleamed.

Lief backed away from the doorway, his heart thudding violently.

Then suddenly, shockingly, the silence of the palace was shattered by a hideous chorus of sounds—the high-pitched squeals of terrified horses, Jasmine's scream and Barda's roar, the wild screeching of Kree and, rising over all, a ferocious, ear-splitting wail that chilled the blood.

4 – Attack

Drawing his sword, Lief plunged through the darkness of the library, out into the hallway and on into the entrance hall. As he threw himself against the tall front doors and heaved at the iron bar that sealed them, he heard shouts from deep within the palace.

Help was on its way, but he could not wait. He sprang heedlessly outside, almost tripping over the bodies of the night guards sprawled lifeless at the top of the stairs.

The sun was rising, casting a weird red glow over the palace lawn where Honey, Bella and Swift reared, squealing, their eyes rolling in terror. All three horses were lame, and covered in wounds that streamed with blood.

And shoulder to shoulder, stumbling backwards up the stairs, Barda and Jasmine were fighting for their lives.

31

A vast, hideous beast was lunging at them from below, driving them upward step by step. Its face was the face of a huge, snarling dog, but hideously smooth and glistening. The shapeless black mass of its body rippled like water, and from it writhed hundreds of long, razor-edged stingers that whistled like whips as they slashed at their prey.

Barda and Jasmine were defending themselves as best they could. Stingers cut through by sword and dagger pattered like ghastly rain on the stairs at their feet. But as the wriggling fragments fell they melted into puddles of oily black liquid that joined together, then rapidly returned to the beast, becoming part of its body once more. And every moment more and more stingers budded from the heaving flesh.

Screeching wildly, Kree was diving at the thing's head, driving his sharp beak into the glossy black surface again and again. Plainly he was annoying it, but still it surged forward.

As the beast turned its neck to growl at the attacking bird, Lief's stomach turned over. For at the back of its head was another face, narrow and ridged, with a cruel hooked beak and burning red eyes.

Pointless, then, to try to attack it from behind—or indeed, to do anything but try to escape. For even as Lief leaped down the stairs, raising his sword, he knew that ordinary weapons could not defeat this horror.

It was a thing of sorcery, like the false dragon at Dragon's Nest, like the phantom that had hunted them on the way to Shadowgate.

The guardian of the south had been expecting them. Again, their movements had been known. Again, they had been betrayed.

'Barda! Jasmine!' he roared. 'The doors are open! Get up to the doors!'

But as the words left his lips, he saw Jasmine fall, blood welling from a wound in her side. The stinger that had struck her held her fast, while a dozen more whipped forward to finish her. The dog face howled and snapped in triumph, flecks of foam spraying from its jaws. The beaked face behind it gave a wailing, unearthly cry.

With a roar, Barda slashed savagely at the attacking stingers. Their tips dropped and melted into puddles of oily liquid where they fell. Lief bounded recklessly down the last few steps, cut Jasmine free and began to lift her.

'Get her inside, Lief!' Barda panted. 'I will try to hold—'

He grunted in agony as three stingers whipped around his neck. Blood began to flow freely from the wounds. The stingers tightened and pulled. As Barda staggered, choking, the beast lunged at him, its two faces howling, stingers hissing through the air like striking snakes.

Leaving Jasmine where she lay, Lief sprang forward, his sword sweeping in great arcs before him. Fragments of stingers fell, squirming, beneath his blade. The severed tips of the stingers that had been throttling

Barda dissolved into trails of black slime. As Barda bent double, clutching his throat and drawing in great, rasping gulps of air, the trails joined into one and slid rapidly to the ground.

The beast shuddered and drew back. The blazing eyes of the dog face met Lief's eyes, then dropped to the Belt at his waist.

'Yes!' Lief shouted, wild with rage and loathing. 'I am the one you were told to destroy! But it is not so easy, is it? It is not so easy to face the Belt of Deltora. Get back—back to whatever foul place you came from!'

The foam-flecked lips of the dog face writhed back from its teeth in a snarling grin. And Lief's heart seemed to leap into his throat as the hideous mound of flesh before him swelled to twice its size, and hundreds more stingers erupted from its rippling black surface.

And the next moment, it was upon him.

He was engulfed in oily, quivering darkness. He could not breathe. He could not see. Pain racked his body as stingers whipped around him, binding his arms and legs, squeezing him in a death grip.

But worse, far worse, was the sickening sound, the ghastly rippling, sucking sound that filled his ears as he was pulled further and further into the cold, jelly-like mass of the beast. His stomach heaved with the vileness of it. He wanted to scream, but his mouth was sealed.

He could feel the beast's flesh twitching and quivering. The Belt of Deltora was burning it. But it did not release him. The blood was roaring in his ears. His chest ached with the need to breathe. His mind was growing hazy. Pictures of the past drifted in a sea of red behind his sealed eyes.

So this was what Ava meant, he thought dimly. This was the fate awaiting me. Death . . .

Not yet, king of Deltora. I am with you . . .

The voice of the topaz dragon whispered in his mind, echoing like a voice in a dream. At the same moment, he felt a jolt, as if the beast enfolding him had shuddered all over. And then he heard a roar like distant thunder, and knew—

Again the beast shuddered. There was a spitting, sizzling sound, like fat falling into a fire. And then Lief felt himself falling onto the hard stairs. He felt the cold, clinging flesh slipping away from him, sliding from his nose and mouth, from his arms and legs.

Air rushed into his aching lungs as he took great, sobbing breaths. The air was hot, and smelled of burning. It hurt him. But it was glorious, glorious!

He opened his eyes. He was lying on his side. The air was dark with smoke. A mighty wind beat on him, pinning him down. There was a blaze of golden light, a thunderous roar, and a wave of heat.

He could do nothing. He could only lie gasping like a stranded fish, staring wildly at the trail of oily black liquid snaking into the shadows at the side of the stairs and slipping out of sight.

Painfully, fighting the buffeting wind, he turned on his back and looked up. The topaz dragon hovered above him, wreathed in smoke, its vast wings glittering in the rising sun. Again he heard its voice in his mind.

What was that foul two-faced thing? In all my long life, I have never seen its like.

Lief tried to speak, but could not. So he thought his answer—the answer he knew to be true.

It is the guardian of the evil presence called the Sister of the South.

The dragon's golden eyes narrowed. And this time it spoke aloud. Its voice was very cold.

'When you awoke me, king, I felt evil in my land. But you told me that the centre of the evil was in the land of the ruby where I could not go.'

Lief wet his cracked lips. 'I did not mean to deceive you,' he managed to croak. 'I told you there were four Sisters in all, and that we only knew the whereabouts of one—the Sister of the East, in Dragon's Nest. Since then we have circled the land, and three Sisters have been destroyed. But one remains, and we have just learned that it is in Del.'

'I knew it was so,' hissed the dragon, dropping a little lower. 'Its song has been tormenting me. I hear it now. It is here, hidden deep in the city's heart.'

. . . the centre . . . the heart . . .

Josef's voice echoed in Lief's mind.

'You feel the evil in the palace, dragon?' Lief rasped urgently.

'I do,' growled the dragon. 'Why else have I haunted this place, braving the weapons of your guards?

36

I do not care for cities, where the air is foul, and humans run about shrieking at the sight of me, like granous in a trap.'

And as it spoke, there were frenzied shouts from the top of the stairs. The next instant, an arrow had flown through the air and buried itself in the dragon's soft underbelly.

The dragon bellowed and rose into the dawn sky. Its dark red blood splashed to the stairs, spattering Lief's face and hands.

Lief cried out in horror, struggling to rise, to shout to the guards to stop, stop! But the pounding wind of mighty wingbeats pinned him down, and his croaking voice could not be heard above the dragon's roars.

The dragon flew clumsily away, slowly gaining height. Spears sped after it, but could not reach it, falling uselessly to the ground. Blood dripped from its wound as it flew. Lief watched helplessly, racked with pain, filled with dismay.

He heard the sound of feet clattering down the stairs. Then someone was crouching beside him. Through the haze of smoke still drifting in the air Lief saw a square, sharp-eyed face surrounded by a frizz of brown hair. He saw the well-worn bow slung over one sturdy shoulder, and knew whose arrow had pierced the dragon's hide.

'Gla-Thon,' he croaked, trying to sit up. 'How—?'

'Be still,' the gnome said gruffly. 'You have lost much blood. Jasmine and Barda too. That vicious yellow beast nearly made an end of you.'

'No,' Lief mumbled. His head was swimming. Shadows were flickering at the edges of his vision.

Desperately he tried to hold the shadows back. He needed to explain. He needed to tell Gla-Thon, tell them all, of the two-faced beast, of the dragon's rescue. But there was something even more urgent.

'Josef. Paff,' he whispered. 'The Toran Plague . . .'

He saw Gla-Thon's small eyes widen. He saw her lips move, as though she was speaking.

But the shadows were closing in. Lief could not stop them. They moved faster, faster . . . And at last all was darkness.

✳

When Lief woke, he was lying in his old palace bed chamber. A feather quilt covered him. There was a soft pillow beneath his head. The faint scents of soap, clean linen and healing herbs drifted in the air. Sunlight was streaming through the barred window, turning the swirling dust motes into flecks of gold.

For a moment he was still, his mind lost in a pleasant haze. Then memory came flooding back and instantly every nerve in his body was jangling.

He sat up abruptly, drawing a sharp breath as pain shot through him. He looked down and saw that the torn, blood-soaked Toran robe was gone, and he was wearing a crisp white nightshirt. At the same moment he realised that while he had been unconscious someone had bathed his wounds, bandaged the worst of them and smeared the rest with healing balm.

With a jolt of panic he felt for the Belt of Deltora. But it was there, around his waist, gleaming against the white of the nightshirt.

He looked around the familiar room. His sword lay in a corner near the bed. Beside the sword was the pack he had left in Tora.

Who had brought it from Tora? How long had he been lying here unconscious? Half a day? More?

Suddenly the silence in the room was no longer peaceful, but ominous.

Lief thought of his mother. He thought of Jasmine and Barda, bleeding on the palace steps. He thought of Josef, his face disfigured by scarlet weals, and Paff, her eyes rolled back in her head . . .

In terror he glanced down at his hands and in shamed relief saw that no red lumps marked the skin.

The Toran Plague had not touched him. Or—not yet.

Painfully he swung his legs over the side of the bed and stood up. The room seemed to spin around him, and he grasped the edge of the bedside cabinet for support. He fumbled his way to his pack, found his clothes and began to pull them on.

His heart lurched as he heard the click of a lock and saw the door handle turn. Without quite knowing why, he seized his sword and stood with his back to the wall, waiting.

5 - A Sad Reunion

The door opened and Doom came silently into the room. He froze when he saw that the bed was empty. Slowly he turned his head till he saw Lief standing in the corner, sword in hand. The corner of his mouth tightened.

'So you have become cautious at last, Lief,' he said. 'Better late than never.'

Lief grinned shakily and threw down his sword.

'Doom,' he said, holding out his hand. 'I am very glad to see you.'

Doom stood where he was. 'I am sure you will understand if I say that I am *not* glad to see you,' he answered coldly. 'Did I not tell you to stay away from here?'

Lief fought down a flare of anger. 'You also told me to continue my quest,' he snapped, letting his rejected hand fall. 'Whether you wished me to see my dying mother or not, I had to come to Del. The Sister of the South is here.'

With bitter satisfaction he watched Doom's face change. Then he saw his old friend's shoulders slump, and felt ashamed.

'Forgive me,' he said quickly, holding out his hand again. 'You could not have known. And no doubt I would have come even if the Sister were not in Del.'

This time Doom moved forward, and took the outstretched hand in both of his.

'No doubt you would, Lief,' he said. 'Your heart has often ruled your head. It is one of the many things that make you a better king than I could ever be, for all your youth.'

As if fearing he had shown his feelings too plainly, he cleared his throat and abruptly released Lief's hand.

'Barda and Jasmine are still sleeping,' he said, in something far more like his normal tone. 'According to Gla-Thon it is a miracle that you are all still alive. Dragons can be deadly allies, it seems.'

Without waiting for an answer, he held out a piece of red cloth like the one loosely knotted around his own neck.

'I know there is no hope of persuading you to keep away from Sharn, however much I might wish to,' he said. 'Tie this mask around your face. It will give you some protection from the infection.'

'Before I see Mother, I must go to Josef,' Lief said hurriedly.

Doom stared at him in angry astonishment. 'You must do as you please, Lief,' he said curtly. 'But if you wish to see Sharn alive, there is no time to waste.'

Fear swept through Lief like a cold wind, driving everything else from his mind, chilling him to the bone.

✳

Minutes later, Lief was standing by his mother's bed, his breath coming hard and fast beneath the stifling cloth mask that covered his mouth and nose.

'Do not venture too close,' warned Doom, who had remained by the door. 'And do not touch her.'

Angry-looking scarlet lumps covered Sharn's face and neck. Her brow was beaded with sweat. Her lips were dry and cracked. Dark grey shadows smudged the skin beneath her eyes. Her breathing was very faint.

Lief's throat tightened. 'How long has she been like this?' he managed to say.

'This is the third day,' Doom answered. 'She reached Del at sunset, three nights ago, bearing the glad tidings that you had been found safe and well, and were travelling on to find the Sister of the South. A troop of guards escorted her to the palace. She spoke to every one of them . . . as is her way.'

He paused, then continued in the same level tone.

'Her belongings were brought here, but she remained below, though she was tired and windswept from her journey. She greeted the crowds of the hungry gathered in the entrance hall and with her own hands served the soup that had been prepared for them.

42

Afterwards she went to visit the stables, then she and I ate in the kitchen with the cooks. At last she admitted to weariness, and went directly to bed.'

Again he paused. Lief waited, his eyes fixed on his mother's face.

'By morning she was burning with fever and the red weals were already showing on her face,' Doom went on after a moment. 'The guards who had escorted her to the palace, many of the people she had served, the horse-master who greeted her in the stables and the cooks who sat with us at table, were in the same state. Most of them died the same day. Then those close to them began to fall ill. And so it went on.'

'How many are dead?' Lief forced himself to ask.

Wearily, Doom rubbed his brow with the back of his hand. 'Many hundreds,' he said. 'I have lost count over the past days. I have given orders that the dead are to be burned. The citizens have all been told to cover their faces in the streets, and while nursing the sick. But still the deaths continue.'

He sighed. 'The only thing I seem to have achieved is to stop the plague spreading beyond Del. No-one is permitted to leave the city. That is why Gla-Thon is with us. A Kin carried her from Dread Mountain, to bring me news of you. The Kin returned at once, but Gla-Thon remained, and she was still here when the plague broke out. Gers the Jalis and Steven were trapped in the same way.'

'Gers and Steven?' Lief repeated stupidly.

'Gers came asking for food for his people,' Doom said. 'Steven arrived a week ago, with the boy Zerry. They told me of your journey to Shadowgate, and your encounters with the Masked Ones, and Laughing Jack.'

Lief nodded, his mouth suddenly dry.

'To me the Masked Ones were just one of Deltora's many curiosities,' Doom went on sombrely. 'I have never known their history, or cared to find it out. I was astonished when Steven told me that the troop was founded by Ballum, the younger brother of King Elstred.'

He saw Lief's eyes widen, and nodded.

'Did Steven not tell you?' he said. 'You share a bloodline with the traditional leaders of the Masked Ones, Lief. No doubt that is why Bess saw a resemblance between you and her son. Steven told me that Ballum was a magician and juggler—much loved by the people, and by his brother, the king. Then a trick went wrong and Ballum's face was badly marked by fire.'

'So he began wearing a mask to hide his injuries,' Lief said slowly.

'He did,' said Doom. 'But not long afterwards he was accused of attempting to kill Elstred out of bitterness and jealousy, and was forced to flee.'

He shrugged at Lief's muffled gasp. 'Yes, it is likely that Elstred's chief advisor planned it all, to ensure that Elstred listened to her alone. Your father and I were separated by the same trick, centuries later. The Enemy forgets nothing, it seems.'

'Ballum was hunted, no doubt, supposedly on the

king's orders,' Lief said, remembering how bitterly the Masked Ones had spoken of the king in Del.

'Of course,' Doom said. 'But he kept to the wilder parts of Deltora, earning his bread as a travelling entertainer, and was never caught. Gradually a loyal troop gathered around him. They moved around constantly, and they all wore masks, so that if ever they were attacked, the guards would not know at once which one of them was Ballum.' He raised a tired hand, and dropped it again. 'Whether Ballum had discovered the secret of making the masks permanent by that time, or found it out later, no-one can know,' he added.

Lief shuddered and turned his head away.

'Forgive me,' Doom said awkwardly. 'This is not the time to be speaking of such things.'

He cleared his throat. 'Steven's story of what nearly befell you filled me with horror, but I was glad to see him—more glad than I can say. Now I wish with all my heart that he had stayed away. If he and Nevets fall victim to this accursed plague—'

'They will not,' said a quiet voice. 'Did you not tell me that Steven and the boy had taken the horse-master's place? They will be safe in the stables, surely.'

Lief looked up and with dull surprise saw Zeean of Tora standing by a second bed on the other side of the room. Like him, and like Doom, Zeean was wearing a mask of red over her mouth and nose. Her hands were covered by close-fitting scarlet gloves of some shining Toran cloth.

She saw him staring at her, and her eyes warmed in a sad smile of greeting. Lief saw with a shock that there was a large, darkening bruise on her cheekbone, just beneath her eye.

'As you see, I decided that I had to come after you, to bring Sharn what comfort I could,' she said. 'Marilen dearly wanted to come also, but her father persuaded her to remain in safety, and I am very glad of that. Del is no place for Marilen now—and not just because the risk of infection is so great, either.'

She moved away towards the wash stand, revealing the person lying motionless in the bed. Lief stared in horror at the strong, handsome face branded by the terrible marks of the Toran Plague.

'Lindal!' he whispered. 'But only last night she was—'

'The Plague works quickly once it strikes,' Doom said grimly. 'Consider the guards on the door last night—healthy when they went on duty, dead before dawn. I found Lindal like this when I came to tell her that you were here, and injured, and that Josef and Paff had been struck down.'

He grimaced. 'And now Zeean has come to take her turn in this chamber of death,' he added. 'She insists upon it, though neither Sharn nor Lindal would want her to risk—'

'They cannot be left alone to suffer, Doom,' said Zeean calmly, dipping a cloth into a bowl of water and wringing it out. 'And you cannot be here night and day.

Who is seeing to Josef and Paff?'

'Gla-Thon was willing,' said Doom briefly.

Zeean nodded and crossed the room to Sharn's bed with the wet cloth in her hands.

'There is little enough that can be done,' she murmured, beginning to sponge Sharn's hot face. 'Cool the face and hands. Be there to comfort, and give water. Hope and pray that the body will have the strength to throw off the pestilence.'

Lief wet his lips. 'I had hopes that the diamond in the Belt might help Mother,' he said huskily. 'Now, I fear the help may have come too late.'

Zeean hesitated. 'You may be right,' she said gently, at last. 'Sharn has clung to life far longer than anyone else, but it is a cruel illness, this thing they call the Toran Plague.'

Lief saw her mouth tighten beneath the mask.

'Doom himself came to the city gates to escort me through the city,' she said. 'I think that if he had not, harm would have come to me. The very sight of me—of my Toran robe—seemed to inflame the people in the streets. They called and jeered. Some threw stones.'

Thoughtfully she lifted a gloved hand to the bruise on her cheek.

'Oh, Zeean!' Lief muttered in dismay. 'I am so—'

'I do not mind for myself,' Zeean broke in, moving back to the wash stand, putting aside the cloth and picking up Sharn's silver-topped jar of soothing cream. 'I mind only that your people believe that this evil has come to them from Tora, when I know it cannot be so.'

'It *must* be so, Zeean,' Doom said firmly. 'Sharn came here directly from Tora, and there is no doubt that the plague came with her. Perhaps she was protected from its effects while she stayed within the magic city's walls, but once she left—'

Zeean shook her head, her eyes fixed determinedly on the lid she was removing from the jar. 'If the seeds of such an evil had been within Sharn in Tora, we would have known,' she said.

'I beg you not to say that outside this room,' Doom answered gravely. 'From what I hear, it is exactly what the people of Del suspect.'

'What *can* you mean?' Zeean demanded, looking at him at last.

In dismay Lief saw Doom draw a yellow notice from his pocket and hold it out to her.

Zeean was certain to find out at last, in any case, Lief told himself, as with sinking heart he watched Zeean take the yellow paper and begin to read. I can only hope that she can be persuaded not to tell her people. If food ships do begin arriving on the west coast now the Bone Point Light is restored, Del will desperately need Tora's goodwill.

Gritting his teeth, he turned his back on his companions and shut their voices from his mind. Slowly he unclasped the Belt of Deltora.

Zeean was frowning over the yellow paper. Doom was watching her. Neither of them saw Lief take the Belt from his waist and place it on his mother's chest, with the great diamond over her heart.

And neither of them saw him stare, astounded, at what happened then.

It was as if a thunderbolt had struck him. He stopped breathing. The blood rushed to his face. For a moment he stood motionless, unable to believe what he was seeing. Then, slowly, he lifted his arms.

'Lief!' bellowed Doom, suddenly looking around. 'Lief, no! What are you doing?'

For Lief was pulling the red mask from his face.

6 – Life and Death

L ief glanced at Zeean and Doom, who were both rigid with shock. Then he turned back to his mother and put his fingers to her wrist. Already the faint pulse was strengthening.

'Do not fear,' he said. 'There is no infection here.'

'Are you mad, Lief?' exploded Doom. 'Replace your mask! Make haste!'

Lief did not move. Doom ran his fingers through his hair in despair.

'What have you done?' he groaned. 'Paff was in this room without a mask for only a moment, but still she caught the plague—and passed it on to Josef!'

Lief shook his head. 'I saw Josef,' he said softly. 'I knelt by his chair and spoke to him. Yet I have not fallen ill with the thing you call the Toran Plague.'

'But when did you see Josef?' cried Doom, astounded.

'Before the beast on the stairs attacked,' Lief said. 'No-one knew of it, Doom. And that is why I have not fallen ill.'

'What do you mean?' Zeean asked sharply.

'I mean that there is no such thing as the Toran Plague,' Lief said. 'All the illness, all the deaths, have been caused by poison.'

Zeean gasped. Doom snorted in disbelief. But Lief knew he was right. The evidence was before his eyes.

'You know that the amethyst in the Belt pales in the presence of poison,' he said quietly. 'Look here!'

He pointed to the great gem, which was pale as lavender water, and saw Doom go white to the lips.

Zeean hurried to the bed and bent over Sharn. 'The red marks are fading!' she exclaimed.

'They always fade as death approaches,' Doom said tightly. 'An hour or two after death, there are no marks at all.'

Zeean shook her head. 'Sharn is not dying. She is recovering! The fever is cooling. How . . .?'

Her eyes turned to the Belt. 'The emerald,' she breathed. 'Antidote to poison.'

Lief nodded. 'It saved Barda once. Now it will save Mother. Lindal, too. And Josef. And all those others who suffer, if I can reach them in time.'

Slowly Zeean straightened. Then, very deliberately, she set down the jar of cream, pulled the red mask from her face and stripped the gloves from her hands.

'This is much better,' she murmured. Briskly she

51

picked up the jar again and began smoothing cream on Sharn's lips.

'You are both making a terrible mistake,' Doom said harshly. 'Sharn cannot have been poisoned! She ate and drank nothing I did not share. She did not touch her water jug in the night—that was the first thing I looked at when I could not wake her in the morning. And everyone close to her has fallen ill!'

'Except you, Doom,' Lief said in a level voice. 'Why are you still standing?'

He would not have thought it possible for Doom to become paler, but it happened before his eyes.

'What are you suggesting?' Doom whispered.

Lief smiled ruefully. 'Only that you are so wary, sleep so little, and are so careful of your food and drink, that it would be almost impossible to poison you. Others who spent time with Mother are a different story.'

He shrugged. 'A troop of guards shares the same water vat. Families eat together. Groups of the hungry are served from the same pot. Such people were easy victims for a killer who wanted to mimic the effects of a plague. As were Josef and Paff, who both use the same tin of tea in the library kitchen.'

Doom was shaking his head. 'How could a poisoner enter so many homes and move around the palace—even into this room—without being seen?'

But Lief was remembering a trail of liquid evil sliding into the shadows of the palace stairs. He was imagining it oozing beneath doors, slipping through keyholes, pooling like a living shadow in dark corners unnoticed, unsuspected.

'Something evil is living in the palace,' he said in a low voice. 'A thing of sorcery. I have seen it.'

Doom and Zeean stared at him, then looked at one another uncertainly. Perhaps they wondered if he had taken leave of his senses.

And, indeed, Lief's head was spinning. The urgent thoughts that were flashing into his mind one after the other were threatening to overwhelm him.

Drawing fresh power from the Sister of the South, the guardian would recover and try to kill him again, that was certain. And the killing of others would continue at the same time. The false 'plague' had begun for one, simple reason, Lief was sure of that. But the guardian had quickly seen that it served other purposes as well.

There was no doubt: while the fearful, secret song of the Sister of the South rang on unchecked, its guardian would remain a threat to every living being in Del.

I must get the Belt to Josef so that he can tell me what he knows, Lief thought. Then I must call the topaz dragon back, so we can face the Sister together. I must act quickly, before the guardian regains strength. But what of Lindal, Paff, and all the others who need the emerald's power? Must I leave them suffering and dying?

He grew ever more panic-stricken as his thoughts ran on and on.

He had to warn the people of Del to beware of poison. Food would have to be thrown away—precious food, while people were starving! He had to make the palace guards understand that the topaz dragon was not a threat . . .

So many things to be done at once! And there was no time to waste—no time!

He looked down at his mother. The red marks on her face had still not faded completely, but she was breathing evenly. The power of the emerald had been working upon her for many minutes. He was sure that Barda had recovered in less time. Was it safe to remove the Belt now?

It will have to be, Lief thought grimly. Smothering his doubts, he snatched up the Belt of Deltora and hurried across the room to Lindal's bed.

As he bent to put the Belt down, however, he became aware that something within him had changed. His racing heart had slowed. The feeling of panic was ebbing away.

He glanced at the Belt, heavy in his hands, and saw that his fingers were gripping the golden topaz, the water-pale amethyst.

He had not thought he needed their help. He had thought he was simply facing the truth. Now he saw that the most important truth of all had been driven from his mind by fear.

This was a puzzle, like any other, he thought in dull surprise, as he spread the Belt over Lindal. I almost failed to solve it. Panic almost conquered me. But now I know what must be done—or at least how to begin.

'Not *I*, but *we*,' he said aloud. 'I am not alone.'

'Of course you are not!' exclaimed Zeean. 'What—?'

She broke off with a startled cry as the door crashed open. Barda strode into the room, his throat bandaged and his eyes wild. Jasmine was behind him, vainly trying to hold him back.

'Lindal!' Barda said huskily. 'Is it true—?' He caught his breath as he saw Lindal lying unconscious in the bed.

'She will survive, Barda,' Lief said quickly. 'Josef, too. The Belt—'

'Josef is dead,' Barda said, his lips barely moving.

A chill settled on Lief's heart. Zeean gave a low cry. Doom's face darkened.

'Dead?' Lief whispered. He could not believe it. Somehow he could not imagine a world without Josef in it.

'Steven told us of it, just now,' Jasmine said, tears shining in her eyes. 'Josef died peacefully, not long ago, with Ranesh by his side.'

'Ranesh is here?' Zeean murmured.

Jasmine nodded. 'Manus came with him. They had no trouble in the streets, for no-one could tell by their looks that they came from Tora.'

'But I warned them to stay away!' exploded Doom, clenching his fists. 'Are they mad?'

'Only if love and loyalty can be considered madness!' Jasmine said sharply. 'If you did not want

Ranesh to come to Del, why did you tell him that Josef was ill?'

'I did not tell him!' Doom answered, just as sharply. 'I, at least, have not lost my senses!'

'I fear the fault is mine,' Zeean said.

Doom swung round to her. She met his furious eyes calmly.

'My heart was heavy after my arrival,' she said. 'Torans share their thoughts, but the distance between us now is too great for that to be possible. So I wrote to Marilen telling her of Josef's illness, the attack on Lief, Barda and Jasmine and . . . everything else.'

Doom scowled, and Lief could well understand why. He knew that his own face must show his dismay.

Plainly, all in Tora now knew that the people of Del blamed them for the so-called 'plague', and that Zeean had been attacked in the streets.

'And how did you send your letter, may I ask?' Doom asked coldly. 'The messenger birds are kept under guard.'

The corners of Zeean's mouth tilted in a thin smile. 'You have forgotten, I think, that the bird Ebony came with me from Tora. *She* carried my message.'

Doom cursed under his breath.

Zeean lifted her chin. 'It seems you would rather my people were kept ignorant of things they have every right to know,' she said icily.

'Stop this, I beg you!' Lief exclaimed, unable to keep silent any longer. 'Do you not see? This is what the guardian of the south *wants*! The guardian *wants* distrust between Del and Tora—perhaps only to create fear and confusion, perhaps to stop supplies coming from the west, should food ships ever arrive.'

Neither Doom nor Zeean answered.

Lief flung out his hands desperately. 'While we fight we can do nothing,' he said. 'And we must act quickly, before the guardian regains strength enough to stop us. We know that the Sister of the South is somewhere in the palace—'

Jasmine drew a quick breath, Zeean's eyes widened, and even Barda looked up, suddenly alert.

'The Sister is in the palace,' Lief repeated. 'Josef knew where, I think, but he is beyond telling us now. He may have left us a clue, and the topaz dragon will aid us also. I will summon it as soon as—'

'Summon that menace?' Doom growled. 'You cannot—'

'Listen to me!' Lief begged. 'There is much you do not understand. We must meet with Gla-Thon, Steven, Ranesh, Gers and Manus at once. When they are with us, I will explain everything.'

He saw Doom's face harden into the familiar, stubborn lines of suspicion and leaned forward urgently.

'Once, Doom, when we knew each other far less well than we do now, we stood together in the Valley of the Lost and heard Zeean say, "the time for secrecy between friends is past". Those words are as true now as they were then, I know it!'

The scarred man's eyes met his own. Memories flashed between them. Memories of distrust and heroism, pain and triumph. Memories of plans, of daring, of hope—and even of laughter.

'Secrecy is pointless now,' Lief said quietly. 'The attack this morning proves that the Shadow Lord knows full well where we are. How, I cannot imagine, but clearly it is so. Fate has decreed that the friends we trust the most are here. We must ask them to help us.'

Doom bowed his head. He did not look up as Zeean stepped forward and placed her hand on his arm. But, slowly, he nodded.

'I will gather the others,' said Barda gruffly. 'Where is the meeting to be?'

'Here, old bear, or it will be the worse for you,' said a slurred voice from across the room.

They whirled around. Barda gave a choked cry.

Lindal's eyes were open. She turned her head on the pillow and looked at them.

'The gathering must be here,' she repeated. 'For you leave me out of it at your peril and I fear that—just at the moment—walking is quite beyond me.'

7 - Old Friends

Not long afterwards, a strange meeting was held in the lady Sharn's bed chamber. As Sharn herself lay lost in sleep, the Dread Gnome Gla-Thon, Steven of the Plains, Zeean of Tora, Manus of Raladin, Gers of the Jalis, Doom, Barda and Jasmine gathered around the bed of Lindal of Broome and listened as Lief told them everything.

Only Ranesh had failed to join them. He had flatly refused to leave Josef's side. No entreaties could move him, and at last Barda had been forced to leave him where he was.

When Lief had finished speaking, there was a long silence. Everyone had believed in the Toran Plague so completely that it was hard for them to accept the truth. And all except Barda, Jasmine and Zeean found it even more difficult to accept that an evil presence prowled the palace.

At last Steven cleared his throat. 'Are you saying that this guardian of the south is an Ol?' he growled, his golden eyes flickering dangerously brown. 'I thought the Belt had rid Deltora of those slimy, shape-changing creations of—'

'The guardian is no Ol,' Lief cut in quickly. 'The guardian is a human with powerful gifts of sorcery. The two-faced beast, and the black slime I saw sliding away into the palace, are merely forms the guardian finds . . . convenient.'

There was another moment's silence as his audience took this in.

'If what you say is true, Lief,' Gla-Thon murmured, 'no food or drink in Del is safe.'

'The guardian has been leaving the palace under cover of darkness, but I do not believe the Sister would be left unprotected for long,' Lief said. 'I think the homes closest to the palace are in the greatest danger.'

'Certainly most of the deaths have occurred either in the palace itself, or nearby,' Doom said, frowning thoughtfully. 'It seemed only natural, when we thought of this curse as a plague brought to Del by Sharn. Palace workers who go to their homes each night usually live quite near.'

'Then a circle must be drawn around the affected area, with the palace as its centre,' said Lindal, pulling herself up on her pillows. 'All food within the circle must be taken away. The people there must eat only food given back to them after it has been tested.'

'Folk will not give up their private food stocks without a fight,' muttered Gers.

'I think I could persuade them,' Steven said cheerfully. 'They have grown to know me and my caravan over the past days. The children like my horse and Zerry entertains them with magic tricks.'

He grinned. 'If I load the caravan with food that has already been tested, and offer to exchange it for their private stores, the people will agree in good spirits, I am sure.'

Lief felt a warm wave of relief that was almost joy. Now ten minds instead of one were working on the problems Del faced. And each one of the ten had something useful to offer.

'I do not understand why, after months or years of remaining hidden, this enemy—this guardian of the south—would suddenly begin poisoning innocent people,' Manus said suddenly.

'It did not poison just anyone,' Lief pointed out, taking care not to look at Doom. 'It poisoned Mother, immediately on her arrival in Del. And then it poisoned all those who had come in contact with her, so that it seemed she was carrying a plague. Plague victims are always isolated from others. People who wish to talk to them are kept away.'

'Are you saying that all this began to prevent Josef from seeing Sharn?' Doom demanded.

Lief nodded uncomfortably. 'I fear so. Josef had discovered something of great importance. He would have passed it on to Mother if he could. He trusted her completely.'

'While I was not worthy of trust,' Doom said sourly.

'Josef was addle-headed,' said Gla-Thon. 'I have seen it often in Dread Mountain. Some old ones remain sharp as Boolong thorns till death. Others become filled with fancies. Josef was such a one. He took against you, Doom, because you were firm with him.'

Barda shrugged. 'Addle-headed or not, Josef plainly had important knowledge in his keeping. And now he is dead, and his assistant, in whom he might have confided, is gravely ill.'

'I doubt Josef would have told Paff anything,' Doom muttered. 'He disliked her.'

'If Paff survives, she can tell us one way or the other,' Gla-Thon said. 'And she may well survive, in fact. She drank only half of the brew that Lief says poisoned her, and she has the strength of youth. If she has the aid of the great emerald as well . . .'

'She will, as soon as we have finished here,' Lief said. 'And until she can speak, she must be closely guarded. No harm must befall her.'

Gla-Thon nodded. 'I will see to it,' she said, turning quickly to leave as if pleased to have something practical to do.

'Wait, Gla-Thon!' Lief called. 'There is something else I must ask of you—and of your people.'

'Name it,' Gla-Thon said, her hand on the door knob.

Lief looked at her steadily. 'I need every large emerald from the Dread Gnomes' treasure cave. Every emerald, and every amethyst, too.'

Gla-Thon's small eyes widened, and for a moment everyone in the room could see, flaring in those eyes, the Dread Gnomes' natural suspicion, and love of treasure.

Then Gla-Thon blinked, and the greedy, suspicious light disappeared.

'Certainly,' she said calmly. 'The emeralds to help those who have been poisoned. And the amethysts to test food.'

'Indeed,' said Lief, very grateful for her quick understanding. 'There are some jewels here in the palace, but not enough. Naturally the Dread Mountain gems will be returned as soon as the crisis has passed.'

'Naturally.' Gla-Thon bowed slightly. From one of her pockets she pulled a small bag. She tipped the bag's contents into the palm of her hand and held out a small pile of emeralds, gleaming like green fire.

'I had hoped to purchase food to take home at the end of my stay,' she said. 'Things on Dread Mountain are improving, but the crops are still young. I soon realised my hope was foolish, but now I am glad I brought the gems with me. They will help us make a start.'

'But surely only the gems in the Belt can—' Lindal began.

'Lesser gems are only shadows of the seven in the

Belt of Deltora, but still they have some power, especially in large numbers,' said Gla-Thon. 'The Dread Gnomes have always known this. It is one of the reasons we value gems so highly.'

'My plan is to gather all the sick into one place, and the emeralds with them,' Lief said. 'But the place cannot be the palace, which must be cleared of as many people as possible. I am not sure where else—' He glanced at Doom uncertainly.

'The great food store house near the square is almost empty,' Doom said. 'There is space there for hundreds of beds. Gers, perhaps, can begin the work while I fetch the palace jewels. I will join him as soon as I can.'

Gers grunted agreement.

'Very well,' said Gla-Thon. 'I will see to the gems. I need only a bird to send the message, and the thing will be done.'

'I will fetch a bird,' Jasmine said, moving eagerly to join Gla-Thon at the door.

'Fetch two,' Lief called after her. 'Zeean must write again to Marilen.'

'Must I indeed?' murmured Zeean. 'And what am I to say?'

Lief glanced at her. She had lowered herself into a chair. Her hand was raised to the darkening bruise beneath her eye as if it pained her.

'Your people must be told that the Toran Plague is a lie, and that soon everyone in Del will know it,' he said.

Zeean nodded slowly. 'And what else?'

Lief hesitated. He had planned to speak further to Zeean in private. Plainly, however, she had already guessed the second part of the message and was not going to permit him to keep any secrets.

Perhaps she is right, he thought. Everyone should understand what may be ahead.

'Marilen must come to Del without delay,' he said reluctantly. 'She is the heir to the Belt of Deltora. When I face the Sister of the South Marilen must be here, standing in readiness to put on the Belt should I not survive.'

He paused. The room was utterly still. Zeean had closed her eyes. Everyone else was staring at him in shock.

'Barda and Jasmine will be with me,' Lief went on, without looking at either of his companions. 'It will be their task to take the Belt from me and deliver it safely to Marilen, if they feel the time is right.'

'You have faced three Sisters before this, and three guardians too, Lief,' Barda said, almost angrily. 'Why do you now—?'

'This is the last Sister, and I fear it will be the most terrible, for all the rage of the Shadow Lord will be focused upon it,' Lief broke in. 'And—'

He looked down at his hands. And I have felt disaster ahead ever since I set foot in the palace, he thought. The feeling grows stronger with every step I take towards my goal.

'And the topaz dragon is not merely exhausted, as the dragon of the amethyst was, but injured,' he said aloud. 'It will try with all its might to rid its land of the Shadow Lord's evil. But the effort may destroy it, and without it, I too, am lost.'

Gla-Thon gave an agonised groan. 'Then if you die, the fault will be mine, for it was I who shot the beast!'

'No blame can be attached to you, gnome,' growled Gers. 'You thought you were saving Lief's life. I would have done the same, in your place.'

'And I,' Lindal put in. 'No-one from Broome, which is built on the ruins of Capra, could doubt the treachery of dragons. And so I have been telling all who ask me, ever since I came here.'

Lief did not argue. There was no time for a long discussion about the faith of dragons now.

'All the more reason, then, for Barda to warn the guards that the topaz dragon is to be protected, not attacked,' he said, instead.

'They will not like that,' growled Gers. 'They think they saw the dragon savaging their king. It will be hard to persuade them differently.'

'They will believe what they are told, and do as they are ordered!' snapped Barda. 'If they had responded to our calls for help in proper time, they would have seen the real attacker for themselves.'

He shook his head, scowling. 'I thought I had left them in good hands with Corris, but it seems that discipline has grown very slack.'

'Corris died on the first day of the plague,' Doom said. 'Dunn, his second in command, is in charge now.'

Barda grimaced, but whether this was in regret for Corris or disdain for Dunn, Lief could not tell.

'I suggest we end this meeting now,' Doom said abruptly. 'There is much to be done, and little time to waste.'

There were murmurs of agreement, and soon only Lief, Zeean, Lindal and Manus remained in the room with the sleeping Sharn.

'There are tasks for all but me, it seems,' said Manus softly. 'Is there nothing I can do?'

Lief put his arm around the Ralad man's shoulders. His heart was heavy, but he kept his voice steady as he spoke.

'You, Manus, have the most important task of all,' he said. 'You are a builder of Raladin. Your ancestors built this palace, stone by stone. If anyone can help me find where the Sister of the South is hidden, it will be you.'

8 – Fearful Discoveries

Leaving Zeean to write her letter to Marilen, Lindal to fume at the weakness that forced her to remain in bed, and Sharn still sleeping, Lief and Manus hurried downstairs to the library.

Lief went to the storeroom and quickly found the large, flat wooden box which held the original plans of the palace drawn by the builders of Raladin for King Brandon long ago. As he lifted the box from its high shelf and took it to a work table, he felt a pang.

Josef had often pointed out this box to him, plainly hoping that he would ask to see the plans. But Lief had never asked. He was bored by the whole idea. Josef had only managed to capture his interest once, when he told Lief that the palace had taken forty years to build.

'Forty years!' Lief had exclaimed.

'Indeed!' Josef had said, beaming. 'Brandon moved in as soon as the ground floor was completed, but he did not live to see the work finished. His son, Lucan, had that honour. Now, if you would just lift the box down for me, I will show you . . .'

But Lief had hurriedly made excuses and left the library, promising to examine the plans another day.

Now, it seemed, that day had come. But Josef had not lived to see it.

Manus began taking out the ancient parchments one by one, exclaiming over them in awed fascination.

'Look for secret spaces, especially in central rooms, Manus,' said Lief. 'Josef said the Sister was in "the centre", "the heart". He may just have meant the palace itself, in the centre of Del. But he could have meant that the Sister is hidden somewhere in the centre of the palace.'

Manus nodded vaguely, his eyes fixed on the plans.

Lief left him and went quickly to Josef's room. He tapped the door lightly, looked in and was startled to find the room empty.

For a moment he simply stared in astonishment. Then he realised that Ranesh had almost certainly carried Josef to the chapel, where he could lie in state as befitted a Deltoran hero.

Fighting down the lump in his throat, Lief hurried to the desk. As he reached for the open *Deltora Annals* volume that Josef had pulled over his secret work, his eye was caught by the stack of paper tied with blue ribbon lying on the left of the desk.

He glanced at the top page.

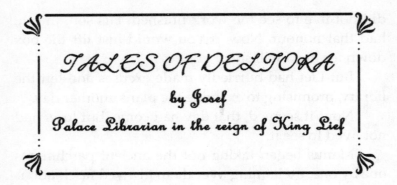

So Josef had finished his book at last. Again the lump rose in Lief's throat. He took a breath, and looked back at the heavy open volume in front of him.

It was Volume 1 of the *Annals*, where all the old folk tales were recorded. Lief's heart lurched as he noted that it was open at the tale of the Four Sisters.

Sickened afresh at the thought of the gloating pleasure the Shadow Lord must have taken in naming his own vile creations after the sisters in the old Jalis tale, Lief lifted the book aside.

And there was nothing beneath it at all. Josef, or someone else, had moved or destroyed whatever had been there.

The disappointment was like a blow. But Lief was shamed to find that deep within him, below the disappointment and frustration, there was a tiny glow of relief. The room would have to be searched—every book and paper in it examined. But for now, the Sister's hiding place remained unknown. He did not yet have to take another step towards the darkness.

He felt numb as he turned away from the desk and left the room.

Manus was still absorbed in the plans and Lief did not hail him. Instead, he walked rapidly to Paff's chamber.

The door hung open, sagging on its hinges. Lief called softly, and went in. Gla-Thon was standing at the end of Paff's bed, bow drawn.

'Ah, Lief, it is you,' Gla-Thon said, lowering her bow and moving aside.

Lief could see at once that Paff was much better. Her body had relaxed. Her eyes were closed in what seemed a natural sleep.

'All the emeralds I had are beneath the covers, close to her heart,' Gla-Thon whispered. 'I put them there the moment I returned. And here is the message to be sent to Fa-Glin.'

She held out the note. Taking it with a nod of thanks, Lief approached the bed. It seemed to him that as he drew closer Paff stirred a little. He felt for the clasp of the Belt.

'If we leave her to recover with the aid of my emeralds alone, we will learn much that will help in the treatment of others,' Gla-Thon murmured. 'It would be a very useful experiment.'

Lief hesitated, then shook his head. 'Josef may have told her something,' he said. 'It is a small chance, perhaps, but the sooner she can speak, the sooner—'

He broke off and swung round as he heard the sound of running footsteps and voices outside in the library. He saw from the corner of his eye that Gla-Thon had raised her bow again.

Jasmine appeared at the door. Her face was deathly pale. Kree was fluttering on her arm, and Filli was whimpering piteously on her shoulder. Behind her Manus hovered, his small, blue-grey face creased in distress.

Lief's heart began to pound. He strode to Jasmine and she reached out for him blindly, clutching the front of his jacket.

'I went to the bird room,' she said in a small, tight voice. 'The guards were gone. And the birds . . . all the birds—'

'Dead?' Lief exclaimed.

'Dead or—or dying,' Jasmine whispered. 'Lief, you must come. You must help me. If they cannot be cured, they must be put out of their misery. They—they are suffering.'

'Stay with Paff!' Lief called over his shoulder to Gla-Thon. And putting his arm around Jasmine, he hurried with her out of the room.

In the centre of the bird room was a living tree, its branches stretching almost to the high, netted roof. Bright sunlight filtered through the tree's leaves, mercilessly lighting the scene below.

All the perches were empty. The straw that covered

the floor was littered with black, feathered bodies, some fluttering and twitching horribly, some deathly still.

Kree hunched silently on Jasmine's arm. His golden eyes looked glazed.

'We will help them, Kree,' Jasmine said. But her face was haunted as she gazed at the birds, many of which she had raised from chicks, and all of which she had trained.

'Poison,' Lief muttered, overturning the water trough by the door with his foot. 'The guardian must have crept in here last night, as we approached Del and while the birds were still sleeping. No doubt the plan was to stop any messages being sent from Del.'

'Where is the keeper of the birds?' Jasmine hissed. 'Where are the guards? Doom promised me the birds would be safe. He swore it!'

'Doom cannot be everywhere,' Lief said in a low voice, unclasping the Belt of Deltora. 'And he has to sleep, like any mortal.'

He knelt by the nearest living bird, and gently pressed the emerald to its breast. Instantly the bird's piteous struggles ceased. It opened its eyes and clucked feebly.

Jasmine made a small, choked sound. She fell to her knees and touched the bird's head.

'There, Blackwing,' she crooned. 'There . . .'

Quietly Lief moved on to the next fluttering body. Briefly he remembered Paff, then pushed the thought from his mind. Paff was recovering without his aid. If she had anything to tell, it would have to wait.

✳

Half an hour later, the sun shone down on twelve occupied perches in the bird room. The dozen birds Lief had saved were ruffled and quiet, very aware of the empty spaces all around them.

'Not one of them is strong enough to fly to Dread Mountain,' Jasmine said in a low voice, as she and Lief stood watching the survivors.

Kree squawked and flapped his wings.

'No, Kree!' she exclaimed. 'You have just flown from Tora. You must—'

Kree screeched, and snapped his beak. Clearly he was determined to go to Dread Mountain, whether Jasmine approved or not.

Lief held out the folded paper. Kree plucked it neatly from his hand and held it fast.

'Go and bid him farewell, Jasmine,' Lief said gently. 'I will not leave the birds until you return.'

Jasmine took a deep breath, then nodded and left the room with Kree riding serenely on her arm.

Lief pushed his hands deep into his pockets and began slowly pacing the room, kicking at the straw with the toes of his boots. Around him, the recovering birds crooned and clucked.

He jumped violently as there was a noise behind him. He swung around, reaching for his sword, as the door of the room opened.

Barda walked in, grim-faced. Close behind him was

a stocky guard with a balding head and an anxious expression that sat oddly on his red, good-natured face. Lief recognised him as Dunn, Barda's new deputy. A red mask hung around Dunn's neck, as though he had only recently pulled it down.

'Manus told us what had happened,' Barda said grimly. 'We have discovered Jarvis, the keeper of the birds, dead in his bed. The bird room guards have been found further down the hallway here. They have not a mark on them, but they, too, are dead.'

'Zon and Delta crawled away seeking help, no doubt, sir, and died where they fell,' Dunn mumbled.

Barda's lips tightened. 'No doubt,' he said curtly. 'But that must have been well before dawn, for their bodies are already cold and stiffening. Why did you not discover before this that the bird room was unguarded?'

Dunn's red face deepened to dull scarlet. 'I have been forced to abandon inspections in this area, sir,' he said. 'We are short-handed, sir, because of the Toran Plague. And the bird room is very out of the way.'

'That,' said Barda through gritted teeth, 'is exactly why inspections are needed here, Dunn. And how many times do I have to tell you? There *is* no plague! Stop using the cursed word!'

Dunn wiped his mouth with the back of his hand. 'Indeed, you said there was no plague, only poison, sir,' he muttered. 'The guards on the city gates have been told, as you ordered, and all of us have removed our masks.'

Unhappily he fingered the red cloth around his neck. 'But Zon and Delta are dead, sir, just like Airlie and Wax, the men who were at the entrance door last night. And none of them were poisoned, I will take my oath on it.'

He met Barda's furious eyes, and glanced away quickly.

'You left the strictest orders, sir, that no guard was to accept food or drink while on duty, for in the past guards have been given sleeping potions by enemies,' he mumbled. 'Zon and Delta were not the sort to disobey, and neither were Airlie and Wax. '

'Nevertheless, somehow they all took poison,' Barda said firmly. 'Get that into your head, and make certain that the other men do the same.'

Dunn's ears were very red. Plainly he thought Barda was wrong. He blinked rapidly, but said nothing.

Barda hesitated, then turned to Lief. 'It is true, however,' he said, looking directly into Lief's eyes, 'that those men were good soldiers. They would not have disobeyed my instruction unless . . . they had very good reason.'

Lief understood what Barda was telling him. He understood only too well. But the thought was hateful to him. His mind did not want to accept it.

Dunn was shifting from foot to foot.

'Can I go now, sir?' he asked nervously. 'The men watching over Zon and Delta will be growing impatient, waiting for me.'

'Be off, then,' Barda sighed. 'But Dunn, try to remember that you are my deputy now. Be considerate by all means, but do not fear the men's displeasure or they will not respect you.'

Dunn ducked his head and hurried towards the door, pulling out a large white handkerchief to mop his brow.

'He will have to be replaced,' Barda muttered under his breath. 'He is far too anxious to be liked to make a good leader of the guards.'

But Lief was not listening. He had darted forward and picked up something that had fallen from Dunn's pocket when the man pulled out his handkerchief.

It was a folded yellow paper. Lief unfolded it and his stomach turned over.

'Dunn!' he shouted. 'Where did you get this?'

9 – The Yellow Notice

unn stiffened and turned reluctantly. When he saw the yellow paper in Lief's hand, his own hand flew guiltily to his pocket and his blue eyes widened.

'Th—There was a whole pile of them on the table in our eating quarters this morning,' he stammered. 'I did not think there was any harm in taking one.'

'There was no harm in taking one,' Lief said, making a tremendous effort to keep his voice level. 'No harm in reading it, either. There would only be harm in believing what it says. It is all lies, Dunn.'

'If you say so, your majesty,' said Dunn. But he did not meet Lief's eyes.

'Is that the Toran Plague rubbish we saw pinned all about the city when we arrived?' Barda exclaimed, glaring at Dunn.

'No, this is something new,' Lief said. 'Very well,

Dunn. You may go.'

Gratefully, Dunn escaped from the room, and they heard him almost running down the hallway.

Lief held the yellow paper out to Barda. 'You had better read this,' he said grimly.

THE TORAN PLOT
THE SORCERERS OF TORA HAVE ALWAYS ENVIED DEL, HOME TO THE ROYAL FAMILY & CHIEF CITY IN THE LAND. NOW THEY ARE PLOTTING TO <u>SNATCH POWER FOR THEMSELVES!</u>

#TRUTH! While our beloved king remains childless, the heir to the Belt of Deltora is the Toran girl Marilen, the puppet of powerful Toran protectors.
#TRUTH! If King Lief dies of the Toran Plague, or is assassinated by Toran spies, <u>Marilen will become queen.</u>
#TRUTH! The new queen <u>will not live in the palace of Del.</u> Her protectors will claim she cannot do so, while Del is racked by famine, dragon attack & pestilence. She will remain in Tora.
#TRUTH! The puppet Marilen is <u>already with child</u>, though she is little more than a child herself. If she becomes queen, her brat will be the new heir to the Belt. It will be born in Tora, & there it will stay. Tora will become the chief city in the land, while Del dwindles.

PEOPLE OF DEL, LET YOUR VOICES BE HEARD!

Let the sorcerers of Tora know that <u>their plot is discovered!</u>
Make them understand that <u>if our king is harmed, we will know who to blame!</u>
Make them see that <u>we will never accept the puppet Marilen as our queen!</u>

Barda whistled. 'This is indeed something new,' he muttered. 'It does not just encourage hatred of Tora. It . . .'

'It threatens Deltora's safety,' Lief finished for him. 'If Marilen does not have the trust of the people, the Belt cannot be strong. Cracks will open in the armour that protects us from invasion by the Enemy. Everything we have worked for will be in danger.'

'Only if you die, Lief,' Barda said bluntly.

Lief nodded. The bright room seemed to have darkened.

Indeed, he thought. And if I face the Sister of the South, I *will* die. This feeling of foreboding cannot mean anything else.

For a moment he stood motionless, his head bowed. He heard Jasmine come back into the room, and the rustle of paper as Barda passed her the yellow notice, but he did not move or speak.

Concentrate on the matter at hand for now, he was telling himself. There is still time to decide whether to face the Sister or not. When you know where it is. When . . .

'These notices are not being written by a citizen of Del,' he said in a low voice. 'They are the work of the guardian of the south.'

He looked up. Jasmine had lifted her eyes from the notice and was staring at him in amazement. Barda, however, was slowly nodding.

'Do you not see, Jasmine?' Lief went on. 'Raising hatred of my heir is the perfect way to make me fear risking my life by attacking the Sister of the South. The guardian is a dangerous enemy—subtle, quick-thinking, and very clever.'

'It is someone we all know and trust,' Barda muttered. 'It is someone from whom a guard would take food or drink without suspicion, despite his orders.'

Jasmine's eyes had darkened until they were almost black.

'Why do you say the guardian is quick-thinking?' she asked slowly.

Lief shrugged. 'To stop Josef from telling what he knew, Mother was poisoned, and false fears of a plague were created. This led to the idea of raising hatred of Tora. Then the guardian remembered that my heir was Toran, and this in turn led to an even better idea.'

He flicked the yellow paper in Jasmine's hand.

'There is such a thing as being too clever,' Barda said. 'These notices will be our hidden enemy's undoing. Sorcery may have been used to copy them in large numbers, but the yellow paper is real enough. I will order a search, and if we find a stock of it hidden in someone's chamber, we will know . . .'

Lief nodded. He took the notice from Jasmine, feeling as if his arm and hand were weighed down by stones.

'I must show this to Zeean,' he said. 'I cannot risk her seeing it by accident, as we did. And I must tell her that there is no bird fit to carry a message to Tora.'

'It is fortunate that there is not,' Barda said, with a grim smile. 'It would be folly for Marilen to show her face in Del now—even if her father would allow her to come.'

'Marilen can surely do as she likes!' Jasmine exclaimed. 'She is a married woman now. And her husband, the father of her child, is here.'

'Perhaps he is,' Barda said, with a shrug. 'But Marilen is a Toran, Jasmine. Her father has great influence over her. And if the Torans felt coldness towards Del before, it is nothing to what they will feel if they suspect that people believe this latest notice.'

He grimaced. 'The strange thing is,' he said, 'what the notice says makes good sense. Tora *has* always envied Del its favoured place in the land. Marilen *is* heir to the Belt. She *does* have powerful protectors. She *is* with child—'

'But—but you almost sound as if you *believe* that Tora is plotting against us, Barda!' Jasmine cried passionately.

Barda's face grew stern. 'I am saying only that we should keep our minds open,' he said. 'And from this moment, we should trust no-one but ourselves.'

Hurrying up the stairs soon afterwards, Lief heard the sound of stumbling feet and laboured breaths from above. He looked up and saw a hand grasping the curving railing of the staircase, high above his head.

His heart in his mouth, he pounded upward till at last he came upon Lindal, huddled on the stairs.

'Thank the heavens!' she gasped. 'I could go no

further. Lief—I fear you have made a terrible mistake. Zeean is deathly ill. And Sharn . . . is sinking. But it was not poison. They ate nothing, drank nothing . . .'

Lief ran. He ran with no thought in his mind at all.

The door to his mother's bed chamber was wide open. As he rushed into the room he saw at a glance the red marks again bright on Sharn's face. He saw Zeean lying back in her chair, sweat gleaming on her brow, her cheeks, chin, neck and arms covered with the same scarlet swellings.

Panic-stricken, he lifted Zeean and carried her to his mother's bed. He put her down beside Sharn, then tore the Belt of Deltora from his waist and stretched the Belt's gleaming length over the two of them.

The amethyst gleamed pale pinkish-mauve, tormenting him.

The amethyst calms and soothes, Lief thought wildly. And it loses colour near poisoned food or drink. What mistake could I have made?

'The amethyst calms and soothes . . .' he repeated aloud.

And, abruptly, the rest of the words came to him, just as he had first seen them in *The Belt of Deltora*.

✝ **The amethyst calms and soothes. It changes colour in the presence of illness, loses colour near poisoned food or drink . . .**

The words Lief had forgotten flamed in his mind.

83

It changes colour in the presence of illness . . .

His heart gave a sickening thud. Wildly he looked again at the amethyst. But surely it had paled, not merely changed colour! Surely . . .

They ate nothing, drank nothing . . .

His mind was roaring, struggling in the grip of a nightmare more terrifying than any he had ever faced.

He had been wrong. The birds had been poisoned, certainly, but the people had not. All along, the amethyst had been reacting to illness, not to poison. The Toran Plague was real.

In horror he thought of Kree, flying to Dread Mountain. There was no other bird to send after him. And the emeralds the gnomes sent would be useless. It was not the emerald, the antidote to poison, that had revived Lindal and aided Sharn. It had been the strength of the diamond beside it that had helped them—for a time.

Every plan he had made was pointless. Everything he had said at the meeting had been based on a terrible mistake.

The meeting . . .

Lief buried his face in his hands.

Zeean had removed her mask because she had believed in him. Jasmine, Barda, Doom, Manus, Steven, Gers and Gla-Thon had all gathered in this room unprotected—because they had believed in him.

And what of the guards even now carrying Zon and Delta away? What of all their comrades, forced by

Barda to remove their masks?

I have killed them all, Lief thought despairingly. And I have killed myself. The diamond would have protected me from the pestilence, no doubt, if I had taken ordinary care. But . . .

But he had taken no care. He had exposed himself recklessly to infection. The plague was surely within him, and sooner or later it would show itself.

The plague works quickly once it strikes.

Not so quickly for him, perhaps. The diamond's power would keep him alive for a time. He would live to see the deaths of his mother, of Zeean, of Jasmine, Barda, Doom . . . all those he loved and had betrayed.

But he would never now face the Sister of the South. He would not die fighting, but sweating in the grip of pestilence. Then Marilen would have to claim the Belt.

Shakily, Lief pulled out the yellow notice and read the final lines.

Make them understand that if our king is harmed, we will know who to blame!

Make them see that we will never accept the puppet Marilen as our queen!

As he read, as he faced what already he knew, cold dread pierced his heart.

This was the disaster Ava had predicted. *This* was the doom he had felt looming ahead from the moment he entered the palace.

He had thought he could decide whether to take

the final step or not. But the final step had been taken long ago, without his knowing it. It had been taken the moment he pulled the red mask from his face and announced that the Toran Plague was a lie.

He had delivered Deltora into the Shadow Lord's hands. He alone.

'Lief . . .'

Lief's head jerked up. Zeean's eyes were open. She was looking at him.

'We were wrong, it seems,' she said softly, trying to smile.

Lief's heart felt as if it was being squeezed by a giant hand.

'Zeean, I am sorry,' he choked. 'I truly believed—'

'Lief, listen to me,' Zeean whispered. 'I am old. I have seen much, and I know. One mistake cannot ruin a life, or a kingdom. It is what is done *after* that mistake, that decides. Remember the lessons of history. Despair is the enemy. Do not let it defeat you . . .'

Her voice trailed away. Her eyes closed.

Lief stared down at her. The red marks were fading from her face. Either the diamond was strengthening her a little, or she was dying.

Despair is the enemy. Do not let it defeat you . . .

'I am already defeated,' Lief murmured. 'Everyone is dying, Zeean. Everyone who trusted me. There is no-one . . .'

Then he remembered. There was one person left— the very person who might . . .

86

Slowly he picked up the Belt of Deltora, and clasped it once again around his waist. He touched Zeean's cheek. He bent and kissed his mother's brow.

Then he left the room, without looking back.

10 – Voices of the Dead

L indal was still crouched on the stairs where Lief had left her. She raised her head as he passed, but she did not speak, and Lief did not stop. He reached the bottom of the stairs without meeting another soul. The entrance hall was also deserted. It was as if the palace was empty of life.

People could not have fallen ill so soon, Lief told himself. They are all somewhere else, carrying out our plans, that is all. But at the same moment, horrible pictures flashed into his mind.

He imagined Gla-Thon crumpled beside Paff's bed, Doom groaning amid a tangle of useless jewels, and Manus slumped over the palace plans. He imagined Steven writhing on the seat of his caravan, while his savage brother Nevets raged within him and Zerry cried out in terror. He imagined terrified guards backing away from Barda's plague-marked body, pulling masks back over their faces, too late. And Jasmine, lying helpless among her beloved birds.

A hollow ache began deep within him.

Despair is the enemy. Do not let it defeat you . . .

He made his way to the flight of steps that led down to the chapel. He stumbled down the steps and pushed the chapel door open.

Josef's body lay on the marble platform, dressed in the traditional velvet tunic and white gloves of a palace librarian. Candles burned around him.

Ranesh was kneeling beside the platform. He turned quickly as the door opened. His mouth and nose were covered by a red mask, and he was also wearing white gloves.

Lief let out his breath in a shuddering sigh of relief.

It was as he had hoped. Alone and grieving here, forgotten by all, Ranesh had not heard the tale that the plague was a lie. He was almost certainly the only person in the palace who had not removed his mask. By a strange accident of fate, he alone had some chance of safety.

Lief stepped into the ring of candlelight and looked down at Josef.

The old man's face was peaceful. The furrows of suffering had been smoothed away. The scarlet marks of the Toran Plague were gone.

Ranesh climbed stiffly to his feet.

'Josef deserves this honour,' he said, with a touch of defiance. 'He deserves it as much as any king.'

'He does, indeed,' Lief said in a low voice.

Ranesh stared at him. 'You are not wearing a mask,' he said dully. 'Does the Belt protect you from the plague?'

Without waiting for an answer, he turned back to look at Josef.

'I failed him, but he said not one word of reproach,' he muttered. 'When I asked his forgiveness, he said there was nothing to forgive.'

Lief's heart gave a wild leap. He had not realised that Josef had spoken again before he died.

Perhaps even now it is not too late for me to make some use of the last hours of my life, he thought, hope rising within him. I have not yet fallen ill. There is still time to destroy the Sister. If Josef told Ranesh where . . .

'Ranesh, what else did Josef say?' he asked urgently. 'Did he say anything about a paper on his desk?'

Ranesh shook his head. 'Every word was an effort. We had but a few moments, and he spoke only of private matters.'

'Tell me!' Lief insisted. 'Ranesh, I beg you.'

Ranesh set his lean jaw. 'He said he wanted to be laid to rest in the tunic of his office. He told me that all his personal possessions were to be mine except for the manuscript of his new book, which was to be presented to you. And . . . that was all.'

The tiny pause before the last words rang alarm bells in Lief's mind.

'No!' he burst out. 'There was something else, I

know it. You *must* tell me—'

Ranesh swung around to face him, hazel eyes blazing with anger. 'Josef said I was his son, in all but blood,' he hissed. 'He said he loved me, and was proud of me. And then he died.'

He clenched his fists. 'Now are you satisfied, Lief? Now that you have heard everything, even something that only *I* had the right to hear, will you leave me alone with my grief?'

Lief bit his lip. 'I am sorry,' he said softly. 'But I cannot leave you alone. There is something you must do.'

'I can do nothing,' Ranesh muttered. 'I must watch over Josef till dawn tomorrow, as is the palace way. You must ask someone else to run your errands.'

Lief clenched his own fists. 'By dawn tomorrow, every person in the palace will be dead, Ranesh,' he said in a level voice. 'The plague will have finished them. I may still be alive, but I will be so feeble that I will be useless. You are the only one who can do what must be done.'

As Ranesh gaped at him in horror, he pulled the yellow notice from his pocket and held it out.

'You must take a horse and ride like the wind to Tora,' he said. 'Show this notice to Marilen, and tell her that it is the work of one who would hand Deltora to the Shadow Lord. Tell her that our land's fate is in her hands.'

Ranesh's face darkened as he read the notice.

'Marilen must come here, despite the plague, and take possession of the Belt,' Lief said. 'She must convince the people that she is not just a Toran puppet, but the true queen of the whole of Deltora. And you must stand beside her, Ranesh. You are of the people, and they know you. Ranesh—'

'There is no need to say more,' Ranesh murmured, tucking the yellow notice into the pocket of his coat.

Gently he touched Josef's shoulder. Then he walked to the chapel door. Standing there, he seemed taller than he had before.

'Never have I been asked to take responsibility for anything,' he said. 'I have been a thieving boy of the streets. I have been the student and helper of Josef. I have been the husband of Marilen. But you have put your trust in me, Lief, and I will not fail you.'

'The guards will let you pass,' Lief said soberly. 'They will tell you that you do not need your mask, but they are wrong. Do not uncover your face until Del is well behind you.'

Ranesh nodded briefly, and was gone.

Left alone, suddenly drained of all energy, Lief sank to his knees beside the platform.

Now he had to spread the word that he had been wrong, that the plague was real after all. Every moment he delayed, more and more people were taking off their masks, exposing themselves to infection.

But he stayed where he was. He pressed his burning brow against the platform's cold marble. The heavy silence of the small, chilly room was so intense that it seemed to make its own sound.

It came to him that his family was cursed—cursed by the wonder that was the Belt of Deltora. The Belt had weighed down generation after generation of kings and queens unworthy of its power.

And suddenly Lief was almost glad that now he would never marry Jasmine, that they would never have a child to wear the Belt in his place.

Any child of mine would come into the world only to suffer struggle, sorrow, fear and failure, he thought. Like me. Like my father. Better—far better—never to have been born.

The Belt hung heavy at his waist. Suddenly he loathed it.

Let it lie here for Marilen, he thought. I have had enough of it.

He seized the Belt and tried to take it off. The clasp resisted his trembling fingers. Almost sobbing with frustration he struggled to loosen it. His fingers slid over the great diamond, the emerald, the lapis-lazuli, the topaz . . . and there they froze. For the next gem in line was the opal, and that he would not touch.

The rainbow stone could give glimpses of the future. And he did not want to see the future. He could not bear it.

He remembered that only one of Deltora's last seven dragons remained locked in enchanted sleep—the dragon of the opal, the dragon of hope. It is an omen, he thought. Now the opal dragon may never again fly Deltora's skies. Just as hope may be lost to us forever.

The topaz warmed beneath his fingertips. And suddenly the chapel was filled with shadows, drifting around him like smoke.

✝ **The topaz is a powerful gem, and its strength increases as the moon grows full . . . It has the power to open doors into the spirit world . . .**

Lief began to shiver. Tonight it will be full moon, as it was the night we burned the Enemy's crystal, the night this all began, he thought. The spirits of my ancestors came to me then, to aid me. Now they come to me again, but this time . . .

Spirit voices began echoing from the marble walls, crying out wildly. Lief could not make out what they were saying. But the misty faces were angry and fearful. No doubt they were accusing him of cowardice and faithlessness. He did not care.

'I *will* take it off!' he roared, tearing at the clasp of the Belt. 'I will *die* free of it, at least!'

And then, among all the shadowy forms, he saw Josef. Josef was holding out his arms beseechingly. His lips were moving, but Lief could not hear a single word.

'Josef, I cannot hear you!' Lief shouted. 'Josef—'

He swung around as the chapel door opened.

A small blue-grey figure stood in the doorway, a large piece of parchment clutched in his hand.

'Manus!' gasped Lief. Quickly he glanced back to where he had last seen the shade of Josef. There was nothing there. All the shadows had gone.

'I am sorry to disturb you, Lief,' Manus said, a little nervously. 'I did not know you were here. I came to see—'

He broke off, staring at Josef's body lying on the candle-ringed platform.

'Ah, how could anyone do such a terrible thing?' he exclaimed, in a completely different tone. 'It is—abominable!'

'I am not sure now that Josef's death was planned,' Lief managed to say, clambering to his feet. 'Manus—'

'No, no!' Manus broke in, hurrying forward. 'I was not referring to Josef's death. I meant this—this great ugly monument here. Abominable!'

He kicked the side of the marble platform violently.

Lief stared, trying to gather his wits. He had never seen the Ralad man so angry. Even the tuft of red hair on Manus's head seemed to be quivering with rage.

'This chapel was one of the first rooms to be completed when the palace was built,' Manus panted. 'It was to be a place of peace—a refuge from the bustle of palace life. And so it was, by the drawings. It was exquisite!'

Again he kicked the side of the platform. 'And then, this monstrous *thing* was built right in the centre of the floor, completely ruining the space! Look at it! High as your shoulder, and half again as long! Ah, that man! King or no king, he was a buffoon!'

Lief's heart had begun pounding painfully. 'King Brandon?' he asked huskily.

'Not *Brandon*,' snorted Manus. 'Brandon had an eye for beauty. This—this *crime* was committed by his son, King Lucan.'

He scowled ferociously. 'The Ralad builders played no part in it, I assure you. They were working on the upper floors of the palace by then. The first they knew of it was when Rufus, their chief, visited the chapel and saw what had been done.'

He flapped the parchment angrily. 'Rufus was horrified, of course. He found the original plan of the chapel—I have it here—and wrote a note upon it to the king, begging that the room be restored to its original state. But King Lucan refused absolutely. Or so his chief advisor said, in the insulting note he wrote back.'

'What was this chief advisor's name, Manus?' Lief asked in a low voice.

Manus thrust the parchment forward. 'See for yourself!' he exclaimed bitterly, stabbing a finger at the words penned beneath the Ralad builder's note.

The King wishes the chapel to remain exactly as it is. Do not raise the matter again.

DRUMM

11 - The Dare

Lief turned away from the parchment and looked down at Josef's peaceful face. So this is what you were trying to tell me, Josef, he thought. The evil is here, in the palace's dead heart, the centre of centuries of grief and pain.

Gently he gathered the old man's body in his arms and lifted it from the platform.

'Lief, what are you doing?' Manus cried, very shocked. 'The platform is vile, yes! But I did not mean—'

But cradling Josef's frail body, Lief was already walking to the chapel door.

'Drumm was chief advisor in the time of Doran the Dragonlover, when the Four Sisters were put in place,' he called back over his shoulder. 'He caused the platform to be built. The Sister of the South is here, I know it.'

'But this is not the centre of the palace, Lief!' Manus exclaimed, trotting anxiously after him. 'It could not be further to the side!'

He gestured behind him at the far wall of the chapel. 'That is the palace's east wall. The Place of Punishment once stood just outside. The Great Hall is above—'

'I know, Manus,' Lief said quietly. 'But still this is the place.'

He carried Josef's body up the steps and placed it gently on the floor of the entrance hall.

'But—but you cannot leave him here!' Manus cried in horror.

'Better here than where he was,' Lief said. He turned to go back into the chapel.

'Lief, wait a little,' said Manus nervously, plucking at his sleeve. 'You are pale as a ghost! Your hands are trembling. You—you are not well.'

'I fear I am not,' Lief murmured. 'I do not know how much time I have left. And that is why I must hurry.'

His shadowed eyes focused at last on the Ralad man's worried face, and he blinked, as if waking from a dream.

'I am sorry, Manus,' he said softly. 'There is no easy way to tell you what I must. I have made a fearful mistake, and all of us will pay for it. There is no poison. The Toran Plague is real.'

Manus took a sharp, hissing breath and clasped his hands over his heart. Lief braced himself for the cries of shock, fear and blame that he knew must come. But the Ralad man bent his head, and when he looked up again, his black eyes were clear and calm.

'What must I do to help?' he asked simply.

For a moment Lief could not speak. Then he put his hand on Manus's arm—so small and thin, and yet so full of strength.

'What is below the chapel?' he asked.

'Why—nothing,' Manus said. 'The outside wall runs down beneath the earth, to meet the palace foundations. The inner wall beside us here continues down to form the first wall of the dungeons below the entrance hall. By the plan, there is only empty space in between—a cavern too small and low to be used for anything.'

'The Enemy found a use for it, it seems,' Lief said grimly. 'Now, listen carefully, Manus. Everyone, except those too ill to walk, must leave the palace at once. Tell them it is by order of the king. Tell them to put their masks back on, go down to the city and spread the word that the plague is real. Then go yourself, Manus. Find Doom, Gers and Steven, if you can, and tell them I . . .'

His throat closed. He struggled to go on, but this time he could not.

'You have not mentioned Barda and Jasmine,' Manus said quietly. 'They are here, in the palace. Do you really think that they will leave "by order of the king"?'

Lief gave a twisted smile. 'No,' he admitted. 'If they are still able to come to me they will, whatever I say. We will stand together against the Enemy, one last time.'

Manus nodded, his eyes very bright, and darted

away without another word.

Lief put his fingers on the topaz once more and silently, insistently, called to the golden dragon.

The top of the platform was a smooth slab of marble bordered by a raised band carved in swirling patterns. Lief wondered if it could be removed. He put his shoulder to the slab and pushed. The slab did not budge.

'You will not shift it that way,' boomed a familiar voice. Lief looked around to see Barda striding towards him, with Jasmine by his side. Over his shoulder the big man carried the vast iron bar from the entrance doors, as easily as he might carry a log of wood for the fire.

'Jasmine and I met at the bottom of the stairs,' Barda said, lifting the bar from his shoulder with a grunt and moving to the side of the platform. 'She had just been talking to Manus, and was coming here, so I thought I would join her.'

Jasmine took Lief's arm. 'The birds are all well,' she said. 'They, at least, *were* poisoned, and the emerald worked to a marvel. Oh, Lief, it gives me such joy to know that they will live to fly again.'

Very moved, Lief looked down at her. She was smiling.

Barda eyed the platform and nodded. 'It seems to me that brute force would best serve our purpose here,' he said. 'It is not an elegant way to solve a problem, but sometimes it is better to cut through a knot than to waste time trying to untie it. More satisfying too, on occasion.'

He tapped the side of the platform with the end of the bar. 'It sounds hollow,' he said with satisfaction. 'Move the candles aside, my friends. We need room to move.'

'Barda—' Lief choked, as Jasmine began pushing the nearest candle holders away.

But Barda shook his head. 'What Lindal did not tell me when I met her upstairs, Jasmine told me just now,' he said over his shoulder. 'We both know all there is to know, Lief, and there is no more to be said. Let us do what we are here to do, while we are able.'

He stood back a little and aimed the bar so that it pointed directly at the centre of the platform's side.

'Stand behind me, Lief, and take hold of the bar. We are going to use it as a battering ram.'

Speechless, Lief did as he was told.

'When I give the signal, thrust the bar forward with all your strength,' Barda instructed. 'Jasmine, keep your head down, and Filli out of sight. Splinters of marble may fly.'

He drew the bar back. 'Ready . . . NOW!'

Lief lunged forward. The end of the bar smashed into the side of the platform with a clanging jolt. The shock of the impact jarred Lief's arms and ran all the way to his jaw.

'Again,' roared Barda, pulling the bar back. 'Put some muscle into it! Ready . . . NOW!'

Again the bar hurtled forward, striking the marble with a fearful crash. There was the sound of falling stone and Jasmine gave a shout of triumph.

Eagerly, Lief craned his neck to see.

The platform's side was cracked, and a chunk of marble had fallen away near the centre, leaving a small, jagged black hole.

'That is what we want!' growled Barda. He settled his mighty hands on the bar once more. 'Ready, Lief . . . NOW!'

The end of the bar battered straight into the weakened spot. A huge piece of marble broke away and fell, smashing on the ground.

'And again!' Barda roared.

Again they lunged forward. And this time, when they drew back, the ground at their feet was heaped with smashed marble, the air was full of dust, and most of the platform's side was nothing but a gaping black hole.

They let the bar fall. It crashed to the ground with a dull, ringing sound. Barda bent forward, his hands on his knees, panting.

Lief's hands were slippery with sweat. Sweat was dripping into his eyes and soaking his hair. He wiped his brow dazedly with the sleeve of his jacket, and realised that his hands were trembling.

The black hole loomed before him, dark as pitch, gaping like the entrance of a tomb. He could see nothing inside it. Fear twisted in his stomach.

Jasmine pushed a candle into his hand. The flame wavered dangerously as he bent in front of the hole. Holding his breath, he thrust the candle forward . . .

Except for a scattering of broken marble, the cavity was completely empty.

'There is nothing here,' Lief called, his voice echoing eerily against the marble walls. 'There is nothing—'

The candle fell from his shaking hand. It rolled twice and then lay still on the base of the cavity. Its struggling flame flickered on the flat, grey stone that lay beneath the rubble of broken marble.

Lief's mouth went dry. He crouched, grasped the dying candle and swept it from side to side, clearing the chips of marble away.

'On the floor,' he said in a low voice.

Barda and Jasmine knelt beside him, each holding a fresh candle. By the flickering light they all read the words on the stone—words still as sharp and clear as the day they were carved.

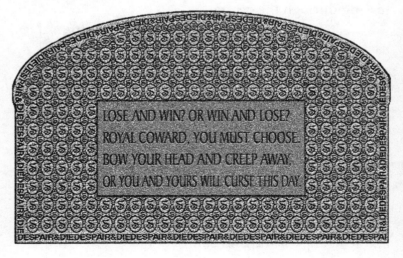

LOSE AND WIN? OR WIN AND LOSE?
ROYAL COWARD, YOU MUST CHOOSE
BOW YOUR HEAD AND CREEP AWAY,
OR YOU AND YOURS WILL CURSE THIS DAY

Lief felt his face grow hot with fury. A wave of trembling sickness swept through him and he closed his eyes, waiting for it to pass. He did not know if the sickness was caused by the evil of the stone or by the Toran Plague. It did not matter. All that mattered were the sneering words on the stone—the words of the Shadow Lord, meant for him, only for him.

'This verse is not like the verses on the stones in the east, north and west,' Jasmine muttered, putting Lief's raging thoughts into words. 'Those others were true warnings, intended for the eyes of any passing stranger. This is—personal.'

'Indeed,' Lief said thickly. 'It is a dare. The Enemy is daring me to look beneath the stone. As once he dared me to look for the first part of the map.'

He remembered the voice of the Shadow Lord, hissing through the crystal.

. . . *this king will never find it. I dare him to try, and go more quickly to his death* . . .

But I *did* find the first part of the map, and I did not die, Lief thought. Then I found the second part, and the third, and the last. And I am still here.

But he knew that the Enemy had planned for this, too. The message on the stone proved it.

Plans within plans . . .

'Smash the evil, sneering thing,' Jasmine muttered. 'Smash it to pieces!'

'Stand aside,' Barda said grimly, getting to his feet and reaching for the iron bar.

104

Lief and Jasmine scrambled out of his way.

And Barda, teeth bared in a snarl of hatred, smashed the end of the iron bar down on the warning stone. He struck once, twice . . . and on the third stroke there was a sharp crack and a brilliant flash of white light.

Barda staggered back, his hands pressed to his eyes. The heavy bar fell, clanging, to the ground. Cracks ran crazily over the stone till the whole flat, carved surface was a maze of black lines. Then, suddenly, the shattered stone fell away, fell with a sound like thundering hail. And all that was left in its place was a yawning pit from which evil poured like a thick, vile smell.

Jasmine cried out and covered her face. Lief fell to his knees and stared. His eyes were watering, but he could not look away.

For down in the centre of the darkness something gleamed—something as beautiful and beckoning as one of the gems on the Belt of Deltora.

The Sister of the South.

12 - Creeping Darkness

Shouts of terror and warning were echoing in the entrance hall. The sounds floated into the chapel, but Lief did not hear them. He was staring down into the pit, staring at the shining thing that lay there.

He could see it clearly now. It was a great gem, grey as the evening sky, but swirling with lines of scarlet light. It was singing to him, singing the song of his land, the song that was part of him, the song he had first heard in the cradle, without knowing it.

It was beautiful, alive, filled with terrible power.

He knew that if only he could touch it, hold it, have it for his own, he could do anything—anything in the world.

I did not understand, he thought, awe-struck. I did not dream . . .

He slid his hands over the marble floor tiles that edged the pit. With his fingers he felt the rough, sawn edges of the wood beneath.

In his mind he saw dark figures cutting through the chapel floor. He saw the shining gem lowered into place, and the stone placed over the gap in the floor, to seal it. He saw the marble platform being constructed, to conceal what lay beneath.

Long ago, so long ago . . . and ever since, the wonder had lain in the darkness, singing the song of its power, and waiting, waiting for *him*.

'LIEF!' The bellow penetrated his consciousness. He stirred irritably, turned to see who had interrupted him.

A frizzy-haired gnome stood at the door of the room, waving her arms at him. Lief frowned. Perhaps he knew her face. He could not remember. But did the fool not realise that he had no time for her ravings now? Could she not feel the power—?

'Lief, you must come!' the gnome gabbled. 'The golden dragon—the dragon I injured—it is flying over the city! It is roaring, breathing fire. Lief—'

Her voice, harsh as the screeching of a raven, broke off. Her face paled. Her foolish eyes widened. She fell to her knees, wrapping her arms about her head.

Lief smiled. Now she feels it, he thought. He began to turn back to the pit.

'Gla-Thon—get away from here!' a shaking voice called behind him.

Jasmine's voice.

Jasmine . . .

Lief paused, a shadow of doubt flitting across his

mind. For a moment he had forgotten Jasmine existed. How could that be?

'Paff is dying,' the gnome whimpered. 'The plague is eating her alive. Her eyes have rolled back in her head. Her limbs have become rigid as stone. I could not lift her. I had to leave her. Then—I saw—the dragon. The people in the city—screaming, running . . .'

Lief swayed. The power in the pit was calling him. He longed to turn to it once more, feast his eyes on its beauty, lose himself in its wonder, and at last slip silently into the soft, thick darkness to take it for his own.

Then there would be no more pain, no more fear. There would be nothing he could not do, nothing he could not have.

But he did not turn. Something deep within him was resisting, holding him back.

What was it? Numbly his mind groped for the answer, and caught hold of that frail, fluttering shadow of doubt.

Jasmine . . .

If he had forgotten Jasmine, what else had he forgotten? What else . . .?

There was a roar like a clap of thunder, and a shuddering thud. The outside wall of the chapel shook.

Gla-Thon cried out in terror.

A soft voice whispered in Lief's mind, hissing through the song of the Sister of the South.

I am with you, king of Deltora. We are separated only by a little earth and stone, and that will soon be gone.

The dragon of the topaz, Lief thought, almost in surprise. It is there, in the palace garden, on the other side of the wall.

He looked down at the Belt around his waist. He saw the topaz, shining like a great, golden star. It was as if he was seeing it with new eyes, as he had seen for the first time, in the Forests of Silence.

At the beginning. At the very beginning. When he thought he knew exactly who he was. When Jasmine and Barda were still almost strangers. When he had no idea what fate held in store for him, for all of them.

He laid his fingers on the topaz, felt its golden warmth.

This was what he had forgotten . . . this. The dangerous, beautiful thing in the pit had almost snared him. It had almost drawn him in, with its dizzying promises of power, glory and freedom from the pain of loss.

And for the first time he saw fully the dark power which had enthralled his enemies, those others who had embraced the cause of the Shadow Lord. He almost understood them . . . Rolf the Capricon. Kirsten of Shadowgate. Laughing Jack. And the unknown enemy here, in Del.

I feel the evil presence, very near, king. It is time to put an end to it.

Lief turned his head towards the wall through which the voice had come. He felt he could almost see through the stone—could almost see the great, golden beast crouching there.

The dragon of Del. The dragon of faith.

Yes, he answered silently. *It is time.*

And his heart leaped as he heard the sound of massive talons raking the earth, as he heard the roar of flame searing stone walls exposed to the air for the first time in centuries.

The mortar between the stones at the base of the chapel wall began to crack. Then there was a scrabbling sound, and the stones themselves began to move.

And at that moment Lief heard a muffled shout beyond the wall. He held his breath, straining to hear.

'It is attacking the palace!' the voice roared. 'It is clawing at the very foundations! Did I not tell you, Manus? This is what the dragons did to Capra! Ah— you foul, deceiving beast!'

'Lindal, no!' wailed Manus faintly. 'Come away! Do not—'

There was a mighty roar of rage and pain, quickly followed by a high scream.

Lief was frozen to the spot, his mind flooded with the dragon's agony, the dragon's anger. He could not move. He could not speak. He could only imagine the blood flowing beneath the point of Lindal's spear, the golden eyes flashing with fury, the huge, spiked tail lashing, crushing and maiming . . .

'Lindal!'

The shout was Barda's. Barda had staggered to his feet and stumbled to the far wall of the chapel. Now he

110

was leaning against it, leaning against the shifting stones, one hand still pressed to his eyes.

'Lindal!' he bellowed. 'Lindal, answer me!'

'Barda, get back!' Jasmine cried sharply.

There was the sound of grating stone. Barda jumped back just as a great gap suddenly appeared in the wall at his feet. Light poured through the gap, blocked instantly by blazing fire, and then by vast talons raking more stones away, and more.

Lief heard Filli squeal in terror. He did not turn. His eyes were fixed on the fiery wall.

The dragon's voice hissed in his mind, cold with anger.

The giant woman speared me. I have dealt with her.

Lief's breath caught in his throat. Instinctively he glanced at Barda, who had backed against the end of the marble platform and was now turning slowly, hands fumbling for the platform's edge.

In anguish, Lief realised that Barda was blind. In anguish he remembered the searing flash of light that had burst from the warning stone as Barda struck it for the third time.

The dragon's voice came again.

Hundreds of people and soldiers are running up the hill—enemies with clubs and swords. I will kill them all.

No! Lief thought back frantically. *They are not enemies. Our enemy is within. Dig deeper. I am here, but the evil is below.*

Through the charred gap in the wall he saw the

flashing golden scales of the dragon, saw earth flying as the vast beast began to dig.

He tried to rise, but could not. It was as if his knees were fixed to the ground, as if the thing in the pit had thrown an invisible web around him, and was holding him fast.

'Jasmine! Gla-Thon!' he shouted desperately. 'People are coming to defend the palace. You must go out and stop them from attacking the dragon!'

There was no reply. And suddenly Lief remembered Filli's scream.

The hair rose on the back of his neck. Slowly he turned his head.

Gla-Thon was crumpled just inside the doorway. Her limbs were twitching horribly.

Plague . . .

But the word had scarcely shaped itself in Lief's mind when Gla-Thon stiffened and jerked onto her back. Then he saw that it was not plague that ailed her.

There was something horribly wrong with her face. Her eyes were bulging. Her mouth was a gaping, bubbling black hole. Her nose was running with what looked like black blood. Thick, black blood was streaming onto the white marble floor.

Lief thrilled with horror. Frozen to the spot, he followed the stream of blood with his eyes. And then he saw, like a vision in a nightmare, someone twisting and thrashing in a pool of surging darkness.

It was Jasmine. A lighted candle still clutched in

her hand, Jasmine was drowning in the black blood that seemed to have a life of its own, that seemed—

Lief moaned aloud as he saw the thick, black liquid for what it was. In the same split second he realised that this was how the guards at the entrance door had died. How Zon and Delta had died.

They had not disobeyed orders. They had not died of the plague, or accepted poisoned food or drink—from anyone. Taken by surprise, mouths and noses filled with clogging blackness, they had fallen and suffocated, unable to make a sound. And then the black slime had slipped away from them and gone on its way, leaving no trace.

'Let them go, guardian!' he screamed. 'It is me you want! Let them go!'

'Lief what is it?' shouted Barda, his shoulders tensing, his eyes staring sightlessly around him. 'What is happening? Lief—I cannot see . . .'

Black slime reared over Jasmine's struggling body, surging towards Lief like a wave. But Jasmine's face was still covered, and Gla-Thon's mouth and nose were still plugged. Lief knew that part of the slime could overwhelm him while the rest remained with its present victims until all breath had gone, all life had ceased.

There was only one thing that would make it leave them, gather itself together in one place. There was only one threat it could not ignore.

He turned back to the pit. He let himself be drawn closer and closer to the edge.

He looked down to where the Sister of the South glowed in darkness. He felt attraction and repulsion, both at the same time.

'I will destroy you!' he whispered.

And, clutching the Belt of Deltora in both hands, he slid his legs over the edge, and jumped.

13 - The Sister of the South

L ief hit powdery earth, and rolled. The song of the Sister was like a knife cutting into his brain. He groaned in agony and curled himself into a ball, his eyes screwed shut. But still he gripped the Belt of Deltora, gripped it so tightly that his hands ached, and slowly, slowly the soothing power of the amethyst, the strength of the diamond, gave him the will to open his eyes.

He was lying beside a stone wall. The outside wall of the palace, he thought dimly, for through it he could hear the roars of the dragon, and the sound of digging. Painfully he turned his head.

There, not far away, lay the Sister of the South.

It was exactly the size and shape of the seven great talismans in the Belt of Deltora, but he could see it now for what it was—a false gem, a jeering copy.

Beneath its perfect, polished surface, beneath the

115

veins of angry red that twisted and flashed in imitation of life, it was cold, dead grey to its core.

Lief stared at it in fascinated repulsion. Now, with the real gems of the Belt warm beneath his fingers, he could not imagine how he had ever desired it. Yet still he found it hard to tear his eyes away and look above it, to the square hole in the cavern roof.

Dim light shone through from the chapel above, but only a little, for the space was almost filled with bulging, oozing blackness.

Lief's heart thudded. As he had planned, the guardian was coming after him, and coming in haste. He could only hope that the threat he posed to the Sister of the South had been enough to make it gather all its forces together, to leave Jasmine and Gla-Thon before it was too late.

He crawled to his knees and then, painfully, to his feet. Above his head ran the huge lengths of wood that supported the chapel floor. There was just enough height for him to stand upright.

He watched the hole in the roof intently, waiting for a black stream to begin pouring to the ground. Behind him, through the agonising ringing in his ears, he could hear the dragon's roars, very near. And he could feel— he was sure he could feel—heat radiating from the stones at his back.

The dragon has uncovered the wall, he thought. It is breathing fire onto the stones. Soon the mortar between the stones will crumble, as it did in the chapel.

The stones will loosen and the dragon will be able to rake them away. If only it can reach me before the guardian does! If only . . .

Make haste! he urged silently. *You are nearly there.*

The only answer was a gust of pain.

And now Lief realised that other sounds were mingling with the dragon's roars. Through the cracks in the wall he could hear roaring voices and the clash of metal.

The guards! he thought in horror. The guards are attacking the dragon.

He wanted to turn, press himself against the wall and scream to the guards to stop. But he knew it would be useless. The men would not hear him. And he did not dare to take his eyes from the hole in the roof, from the crawling blackness that hung there.

He licked his lips nervously. The black slime was moving, rippling downward, he could see it. Why was it not falling?

Then he glanced beyond the hole, at the great beams of wood that made the roof of his prison. And with a thrill of terror, he understood.

The timbers were black with slime. The slime was surging towards him across the roof. It had almost reached him.

With a cry he threw himself to one side. At the same moment, with a harsh, grating sound, a block of stone was ripped from the wall.

Light poured through the gap. Smoky air came with

it, and a tumult of sound—shouting, screaming, the furious roars of the dragon.

And then one voice rose above all the rest, bellowing angrily. Lief thrilled as he heard it.

'Stop, you blundering oafs! Throw down your arms! Get back!'

Barda! Somehow Barda had found his way out of the chapel. He was there, on the other side of the wall.

The shouting died away abruptly. Metal clanged on metal as the guards obeyed their chief's order and cast their weapons aside.

Another block of stone fell away, and another, and another. The golden scales of the dragon, its mighty, clawing talons, almost filled the gap. But still flashes of daylight pierced the dimness of the cavern, dancing on the false gem lying there.

The Sister's glassy surface shone in the light, and its scarlet veins seemed to swell and brighten. Its high, ringing song rose to an ear-splitting wail. Evil belched from it like freezing wind.

Eyes streaming, Lief fell to his knees. He felt the dragon falter. And then, in terror, through the tears that blurred his sight, he saw blackness pouring from the roof of the cavern and forming itself into a bulbous mass, stingers sprouting from it like vines . . .

He knew he was screaming. But his voice was drowned by the wailing howl of the two-faced beast as it lunged towards him, stingers whistling through the air, glistening dog face snarling.

He could not move. He could not lift a hand to his sword. There was only one thing left in his power. He forced his fingers along the Belt till they found the topaz. He focused his mind on the great gem.

Have strength. Make haste. The beast is upon me . . .

The topaz burned beneath his hand. He felt a great surge of power, and with a thunderous crash the last of the wall burst inward.

The two-faced beast howled and screeched as great stones smashed its shapeless body down. And then, before Lief could gather his wits, there was a blur of gold and the flash of mighty talons, and he was raked, tumbling and gasping, out of the cavern and into the open air.

He lay choking, shuddering, half-buried in the dusty soil that the dragon's talons had clawed out with him. He was lying face down, pressed against one of the dragon's forelegs. Its scales felt slippery wet, and he could smell fresh blood. The song of the Sister filled his ears and his brain. It was louder—louder than ever.

And yet—yet surely he was further away from the Sister now. He was out of the cavern beneath the chapel. It was still within. Why . . .?

He forced his eyes open and his stomach turned over. The Sister was no longer underground. It was lying just outside the ruined palace wall, its red veins blazing through a fine coating of dust.

Intentionally or by accident, the dragon had pulled it out of the cavern with him. It was very near. Its evil

119

was battering him into the earth.

And not only him. For now Lief became aware of sobbing and crying, groans of terror and despair. The sounds seemed to be coming from above. Making an enormous effort, he rolled on his side and looked up.

He and the dragon were at the bottom of the great pit the dragon had dug to expose the underground wall of the cavern. Above them, crowded around the edges of the pit were hundreds of people in red masks.

Many were palace guards, but many were not. People had come running from the city, full of courage, determined to defend the palace against the dragon. But now they were on their knees, moaning and sobbing, their hands pressed to their ears. The evil power of the Sister had beaten them down.

Only three people were still standing, huddled together on the side of the hole that was nearest to the back of the palace. They were right at the edge, but, squinting into the sun, Lief could not make out who one of them was. It was someone tall, in any case, standing a little behind the others. Doom, he guessed uncertainly.

But there was no mistaking the two at the front.

The two at the front were Barda and Jasmine. Jasmine was holding Barda's arm. Her hair was whipping in the wind. She was swaying where she stood, and her face glimmered pale as moonlight. But she was alive. Alive!

Alive, only to die of the plague, a cold voice in his mind reminded him. Like Barda. Like you.

He shook the thought away. Whatever was to come, he was fiercely glad that his companions were with him now. He was glad that the enemy who had tried to destroy them was lying crushed and dead beneath the stones of the fallen wall.

If I survive this, I will know at last who our hidden enemy was, he thought. The guardian's true form will be revealed in death. I will know . . .

Now, king of Deltora, while I still have the strength.

The dragon's voice was faint, but still Lief heard it. He knew what was going to happen next. The dragon was going to use the last of its strength to destroy the Sister. It was going to rid its land of the menace that had invaded it, burn the evil thing to ashes.

He pressed his left hand to the dragon's leg, and his right to the topaz. He stared with loathing at the Sister of the South, lying exposed in the dust.

For centuries it had poured misery into mourners in the chapel above its hiding place, and infected with despair the prisoners in the dungeons beside it. For centuries its poison had seeped through the earth into Del, into the Forests of Silence, into the Os-Mine hills, the farms, the shore, the sea, weakening what was good, strengthening what was bad.

Now its time was over.

He felt the dragon gathering its strength. He held his breath, bracing himself for the first blazing rush of heat.

Then he blinked. His mouth fell open and he

moaned in disbelieving horror.

The gap in the palace wall behind the Sister was filling with oily blackness. He could actually see more of the liquid evil oozing from between the fallen stones inside the cavity, and joining the black mass in the gap. The two-faced beast had not been destroyed! It was forming again as he watched.

The black mass bulged outward, spilled onto the earth. The beast rose, vast and glistening in the sunlight, stingers budding in their hundreds from its shapeless body. Horribly, its two faces began to form—the dog face snapping and foaming, the red eyes of the bird face burning with hatred.

But even as the faces were still writhing into being, the beast was charging, stingers whipping the air.

Lief rolled desperately aside as, with a roar, the dragon half-spread its wings and rose on its hind legs to meet its foe. Flame gushed from the dragon's jaws and the rippling flesh of the two-faced beast sizzled, quivered and shrank beneath the searing blast.

The beast howled, but this time it did not retreat. It lunged forward again, stingers slashing at the soft, pale underside of the dragon's neck till the scales were criss-crossed with streaming lines of blood.

The dragon bared its shining, needle-sharp fangs, preparing to strike.

No! Do not bite! Lief thought frantically, struggling to reach his sword. *That is what it wants you to do. It will fill your throat, stop your breath. Do not—*

The dragon faltered, its spiked tail lashing uselessly against the earth walls of the pit. Then it drew back and again it roared, breathing a jet of fire. Again there was a hideous sizzling sound. The dog face howled ferociously as dozens of stingers withered and fell to dust and the flesh beneath them stiffened and burned.

Then without warning, the beast sprang. It surged forward like a great black wave, wrapping itself around the dragon's neck. The dragon tried to free itself, clawing at its clinging attacker, cutting through stingers by the dozen. But the deep channels its talons carved in the oily, rippling flesh closed instantly, and for every stinger that fell, another grew, to join the others coiled around the dragon's neck, cutting and tightening.

The dragon bellowed in agony. Its forelegs crashed to the ground. Still struggling, it rolled heavily onto its side.

'No!' Lief shrieked. At last he managed to grasp his sword, pull it free. Sweat pouring from his brow he staggered to his feet, and threw himself at the beast, slashing at it wildly.

The beast's neck swivelled. The mad eyes of the dog face blazed at Lief. Foam sprayed from its snarling, snapping jaws. And at the same moment, the bird face gave a blood-curdling screech of triumph, and its cruel, hooked beak began to tear at the dragon's throat.

14 - The Battle of the Pit

There was a bellowing roar from above, and the pit was suddenly flooded with blazing yellow light. The head of the beast jerked upward, the beak of the bird face dripping with blood.

Lief heard Jasmine's scream of warning, heard something huge crashing down into the pit behind him. Before he could think, before he could move, a giant, clawed hand had sent him flying.

He landed heavily halfway up the sloping wall of the pit. Dazed, he looked down.

A golden giant with a wild mane of dark brown hair was attacking the beast, slashing its stingers with claws as sharp as knives, tearing its quivering flesh apart.

'Nevets!' Lief gasped.

Through a haze he saw Steven stumbling down the hill of earth, following the deep track carved by his savage brother.

Perhaps Nevets was not affected by the Sister of the South, but Steven clearly was. Yet, sword in his hand, he staggered on, his eyes fixed on his brother.

Nevets and I can not be long apart. We fight together or not at all.

Weak tears sprang into Lief's eyes. So Steven and Nevets of the Plains would die fighting. Well, better that, than . . .

He felt a hand on his arm and looked up to see Jasmine crouched beside him.

'You must get away—to the top,' she gasped. 'Make haste—'

He could see in her haggard face what it had cost her to reach him, but he shook his head.

'I must stay with the dragon,' he muttered. 'For as long as I can, until the plague—'

Jasmine's fingers tightened on his arm. 'There *is* no plague,' she said. 'Lief, you were right all along. It was poison.'

Lief gaped at her. 'But—but Zeean! My mother—' he began.

'There was poison in Sharn's lip cream,' Jasmine whispered. 'Poison taken in through the skin. It was discovered only moments ago.'

Lief's head was spinning. He could not quite take in what he had heard. It was amazing. It was wonderful. It changed everything.

But in one way, it changed nothing.

'Nevets cannot defeat the beast,' he said thickly.

'Whatever he does to it, it will grow again. It will kill him, it will kill Steven, and then it will turn to the dragon. If the dragon has me—has the topaz—there is still a chance it can survive, to destroy the Sister.'

Jasmine held his gaze for a moment. Then she nodded and took his hand. 'Filli is with Barda,' she said.

And Lief understood that this meant she intended to stay with him—indeed, that she had always thought it would come to this.

We fight together or not at all.

He did not argue. He simply gripped her hand, and together they slid back into the pit.

The dragon was still lying on its side, its eyes closed. Its golden scales had faded to a dull, sick yellow. With Jasmine's hand in his, Lief struggled to the massive head, and kneeled beside it.

The dragon's eyes opened at his touch. Lief felt himself lost, drowning in deep, golden wastes of time and space. He heard the dragon's voice, whispering in his mind.

You have returned to me, king of Deltora.

Yes, Lief answered.

You have brought the female with you, the one with the beautiful hair that is the colour of the night.

'Yes,' Lief said aloud. His hand tightened on Jasmine's.

Almost, the dragon seemed to smile.

Do not fear. I am no threat to her in my present state. Nest-making is far from my mind. Who is the golden giant who fights with dragon claws?

'He and his brother come from the Plains, in the territory of the Opal,' Lief said, using words he felt would be understood.

The dragon sighed.

Ah, yes. The territory of the Opal breeds strange beings, so it is said.

The golden eyes closed again.

Strange beings . . .

And suddenly Lief remembered Ava, the blind teller of fortunes, speaking of her brothers, Laughing Jack and Tom the shopkeeper.

As children at home on the Plains we were very alike to look upon, it is said, and our minds could link as though we were three parts of a whole . . .

Another strange family of the Plains. Was this simply chance? Or—?

'Lief!' Jasmine whispered urgently. 'Lief—look!'

Lief turned his head and his heart leaped.

Nevets was still ripping and tearing at the two-faced beast. The golden fur covering his massive body was matted with foam, black streaks and blood. The ground at his feet was littered with twitching stingers and chunks of oily flesh.

Steven was fighting on the other side of the beast, slashing stingers where he could, warding off the screeching bird face as it struck at him again and again.

But something had changed. The stingers on the ground were shrivelling. The lumps of torn flesh were no longer dissolving into black slime and running back to the beast's body, but were drying and hardening where they lay.

'What is happening?' Jasmine breathed. 'It looks as if the beast can no longer renew itself. It is as if . . .'

'As if the sorcery is failing,' Lief said slowly.

His eyes moved to the Sister of the South. Through the veil of dust that masked it, he could see that its red veins had dimmed. And—and surely its song was lower, less piercing than it had been before.

'The evil is less,' the dragon murmured. 'Ah . . . that is better. That is much better.'

Lief glanced at it. Its golden eyes were open once more. Its scales were gaining colour by the moment. The blood had ceased flowing from its terrible wounds. The muscles of its jaw rippled beneath his hand as it relished its returning strength.

'The Sister is dying,' Jasmine whispered. 'But why? Is it the Belt? Steven and Nevets? The sunlight?'

Bewildered, Lief looked back at the fading false gem lying in the dust, and then at the fighting beast.

It was a miracle. Just at the moment when it had seemed that all was lost, the power of the Sister had begun to fail.

And the beast knew it. Confusion and panic mingled with the savagery in the dog face's eyes. The beak of the bird face gaped wide, striking wildly at Steven as if it could not even see his slashing sword.

Steven cried out with pain as the cruel beak of the

128

bird face struck his sword arm, tearing downward. He staggered, clutching the terrible wound. The sword fell from his hand. The bird face screeched in triumph. The dog face slavered and snapped.

And with a thunderous roar of rage Nevets plunged forward, mighty arms outstretched, terrible claws extended, and ripped the beast's head from its body.

For a long moment, the scene seemed frozen. Nevets stood snarling, holding up the glistening, two-faced head to the sun as if offering it to the heavens. The headless mass of the beast shuddered in front of him.

Then abruptly Nevets threw his hideous prize to the ground and stamped on it, stamped it to jelly. And the headless body collapsed like an empty black sack, crumpling into the dust.

Nevets threw up his head and roared, beating his chest. Then, as if suddenly remembering their existence, he swung around to face Lief, Jasmine and the dragon. His dark eyes were empty of thought, burning with the desire to go on killing and killing . . .

'No!' gasped Steven. 'They are friends!'

But Nevets seemed not to hear him. He bared his teeth savagely and gathered himself, ready to spring.

The dragon growled, deep in its throat. Lief reached for his sword and Jasmine raised her dagger.

'Nevets!' Steven shouted desperately. 'I am injured. I need your strength. Return to me, my brother!'

Nevets hesitated. His brutish face twisted as two powerful emotions struggled within him.

'Nevets!' Steven pleaded.

It was enough. Nevets turned on his heel and in two strides was at his brother's side. He took Steven's injured arm tenderly in both his enormous hands. And the next moment, he was no longer a solid figure, but a pillar of blinding yellow light.

Lief could not look at it. He had to turn away. And when he looked back, the savage golden giant with the mane of dark brown hair was gone, and only the golden-haired, brown-skinned Steven remained.

'Now!' Steven rasped, stumbling aside.

The dragon roared, and a plume of golden fire engulfed the dimming Sister of the South. The false gem shone dully in the blaze, then glowed red as a hot coal. Its song became a whine. The red deepened to scarlet and then to a dull brown.

The dragon hissed. And this time the narrow jet of flame that shot from its mouth was white hot. The Sister began to shrivel.

The heat was so intense that again Lief had to turn away. But always he kept his left hand on the dragon's scales, and his right hand on the topaz.

He heard the Sister's whining song rise, rise, and then—stop.

The silence was dizzying.

Slowly, Lief opened his eyes. Where the Sister of the South had been, there was just a tiny heap of white ash, already scattering in the breeze.

'So that is that,' growled the dragon, with great

satisfaction. 'It is over.'

The silence was abruptly broken by noise from above. Lief looked up. The masked people lining the edge of the pit were on their feet, cheering, shouting and stamping.

Towering among them was Barda, his arms raised in triumph, Filli squeaking on his shoulder. Beside Barda was the small blue figure of Manus, jumping up and down as if his feet were springs. Gla-Thon was there, too, bow and arrows still clutched in her hand.

And on Barda's other side was the tall straight figure of Lindal of Broome. Lief stared, overjoyed. Lindal had survived! One of her arms was strapped in a rough sling. She was cheering with all the rest. But her eyes were fixed on the dragon, and in her good hand she held a spear.

As Lief and Jasmine staggered upright, Steven approached them, grinning shakily.

It is over.

Lief knew that this was a moment for relief and celebration. The people above him were delirious with joy. Yet he felt nothing.

'This seems like a dream,' Jasmine murmured, echoing his thoughts. 'At the end, it all happened so fast. It does not seem real.'

'It is real enough. And it was a near thing, too,' Steven said.

'You and your brother did well, man of the Plains,' the dragon said, eyeing him with interest. 'But do not be too proud. By the time your battle ended, the enemy had lost much of its power.'

'Indeed?' Steven said politely. 'Then my brother and I were fortunate.'

Lief was barely listening. He was looking at the drying black scraps that were all that remained of the two-faced beast.

'The beast did not transform,' he said slowly.

'Perhaps it was too badly damaged,' Jasmine said. 'Or it may not have had a human form after all.'

'Perhaps,' Lief murmured. 'But the guardian of the north conjured up a phantom to hunt us on the way to Shadowgate. What if the guardian of the south had the same power, but even greater? What if the black slime was—sent?'

'But surely the guardian would have to go into some sort of trance to accomplish such a feat!' Jasmine exclaimed. 'And the palace is full of people. The danger of discovery would have been—'

'There would have been little danger of discovery if the dread work was done in the dead of night,' Lief broke in. 'And that was when it *was* done—until yesterday, just before dawn, and today, when—'

And at that moment a memory flashed into his mind. A memory. A face. A name.

He shook his head. Surely it was not true. He could not bear for it to be true. Yet as he thought frantically, searching for another answer, many things that had puzzled him fell horribly into place.

'You had better return to your people, king of Deltora,' the dragon said sharply. 'At present they seem happy, but I do not trust them. At any moment they may take it into their heads to attack me again, and I am not yet ready to fight, or to fly.'

Lief did not waste words in argument. The dragon had good reason to distrust the people of Del. And he, too, felt that his place was above.

There was someone there he had to meet.

15 - The Hidden Enemy

B y the time Lief, Jasmine and Steven had climbed out of the pit, word had spread in the crowd that the plague was, after all, no threat. All but a few cautious souls had once again discarded their masks. Guards and townspeople alike were rejoicing.

Steven mumbled something about finding Zerry, and slipped away. Lief guessed that the thought of facing the curious glances of the crowd made him uneasy.

Few, in fact, had seen Steven and Nevets fighting the beast—the dreadful power of the Sister of the South had seen to that. Only a few more had seen the dragon destroy the Sister of the South.

But all of them knew that a great battle had been fought and won, and that something wondrous had occurred. They all felt a lightness of spirit, a flooding joy.

Many kept tapping their ears, or shaking their

heads as if to clear their ears of water. A sound they had always known had gone. For the first time in hundreds of years, the dull, despairing song of the Sister of the South no longer hummed through the air and earth of Del.

Why can I not rejoice? Lief thought for the hundredth time. He gripped Jasmine's hand more tightly. That small, rough hand had become a lifeline for him, a link to what was real, what was true.

He saw that Lindal, Manus and Gla-Thon had disappeared, and that Barda was now speaking to the guard called Dunn. As Lief watched, Dunn saluted, and left Barda at a run, shouting to his men.

The next moment, the guards had begun urging people away from the pit, and back towards the palace gates.

'That will please the dragon,' Lief said. His own voice sounded strange to him—as if it was coming from far away.

Barda was standing alone now—a tall, proud figure silhouetted against the sky. Jasmine hailed him, and he beckoned.

The moment they reached him, Filli leaped from his shoulder into Jasmine's arms, chittering frenzied welcome. Lief took one look at Barda's dulled, vacant eyes, started forward and embraced his old friend.

For a moment Barda returned the embrace. Then, embarrassed as always by shows of emotion, he pushed Lief away.

'Pah! You smell of dragon, Lief,' he said, grinning. 'Keep your distance!'

Then the grin faded from his face. He blinked. A furrow deepened between his brows. He stretched out his arm.

'Take my hand,' he said abruptly.

Wondering, Lief clasped the outstretched hand. Barda blinked again. And then Lief saw that the blankness of his eyes had lessened.

'It is the Belt,' Barda said, his voice trembling slightly. 'One of the gems is aiding my sight. I can feel it!'

And Lief remembered.

✝ **The opal . . . has the power to give glimpses of the future, and to aid those with weak sight . . .**

He did not hesitate. He moved his free hand to the opal. He gripped it tightly.

Instantly his mind was filled with pictures. Grey, barren land. The skeletons of trees. A grey river, sluggish water thick as mud, with huge grey fish lying dead on the wrinkled surface. Monstrous creatures shrieking in the sky. And he felt . . .

Horrified, he tore his hand from the Belt. Panting, he looked up at Barda—at Barda's dark, clear eyes regarding him curiously.

'Was it—enough?' Lief stammered.

'Enough for now,' Barda said. He waited. But Lief's

throat was dry. He could not speak.

'What did you see, Lief?' Jasmine asked quietly.

Lief swallowed. 'I think I was in the Shadowlands,' he said. 'I saw the seven Ak-Baba. I felt . . . a terrible, helpless rage. Burning—' His throat closed, and he shuddered.

'That is what the Enemy will feel when he learns what has happened here today,' said a quiet voice beside him. 'Perhaps it is *his* future you have seen.'

Very startled, Lief spun around and saw Zeean, wrapped in a shawl and leaning on Lindal's good arm. So absorbed had he been in his vision that he had not heard the two women approaching.

'Zeean! How—why—are you here?' he stuttered, as Lindal moved joyfully to Barda's side, exclaiming over his cure.

Zeean held out her hand to show a huge emerald ring that Lief recognised as one of the royal jewels.

'This finished what the emerald in the Belt began,' she said calmly. 'I was able to walk from the palace, with Lindal's help. Sharn is still very weak, so Gers carried her. Doom and Gla-Thon brought Paff, and Josef's body, I think.'

She put her head on one side and regarded Lief and Jasmine's puzzled expressions in surprise.

'Do you not know?' she asked. 'It seems there is a danger the palace will fall.'

'What?' Jasmine cried in horror.

'Manus says that the hole in that foundation wall

means that the palace is no longer properly supported,' Barda said. 'All or part of it will collapse if something is not done quickly.'

He pointed into the pit, and Lief saw the small figure of Manus directing a dozen guards. The guards were labouring to raise a vast pole—a tall tree trunk—in the centre of the hole in the palace wall. They kept glancing nervously over their shoulders at the topaz dragon, who was watching them narrowly, the spines on its neck raised.

And now Lief could see the ugly cracks running up the wall, running all the way up to the long windows of the great hall on the first floor.

'Why *you* are all still standing here, I do not know,' said Lindal. 'Manus told you to clear the area! When I saw you, I could not believe my eyes! Come away!'

But as she spoke a chorus of triumph rose from the pit. The guards had succeeded in wedging the tree trunk into place. Manus looked up and saw the group watching him.

'It will hold!' he roared, punching the air. He turned back to his men, pointed to a second pole lying on the ground, and began giving orders.

'Excellent!' said Lindal with satisfaction. 'Shall we go and tell the others, old bear?'

They strode away, laughing and talking.

'Shall we go also?' Zeean murmured. 'I would be grateful for a chair.'

Jasmine took her arm. 'We will go in the back way,'

she said. 'It is far quicker from here—and there are no stairs.'

In silence they began to make their way to the back of the palace. They walked very slowly, for Zeean's sake, and Lief was glad of it. He was not looking forward to what was ahead.

They reached the kitchen door and helped Zeean inside. A chorus of cheers rang out. Startled, Lief and Jasmine saw that the great table was crowded with people, all turned to them, smiling.

'Why, even Marilen is here!' Jasmine cried. 'And Ebony!'

Lief gazed around at the familiar faces.

Marilen, glowing with happiness, Ebony perched on her shoulder. Ranesh, smiling. Gla-Thon, raising a goblet. Gers shouting. Steven, grinning broadly. The boy Zerry, taller than Lief remembered, his sharp eyes sparkling. Lindal, laughing and banging the table. Barda, beaming, pulling out chairs for Jasmine and Zeean. Sharn, very pale, royal emeralds gleaming at her throat, holding out her arms to him.

Only one was missing.

Lief went to his mother, and embraced her. 'Where is Doom?' he asked quietly.

'He carried Paff back to her bed,' called Gla-Thon, overhearing. 'She has recovered a little, but she is still unconscious. He will be with us shortly.'

'If he has not fallen asleep on his feet,' Gers growled. 'He looks like death walking. I offered to take Paff myself, but he would not have it.'

'No doubt he thought the poor girl was sick enough, without being scared to death by your ugly face, Jalis,' grinned Gla-Thon.

With a roar, Gers swung around, reaching for Gla-Thon but succeeding only in upsetting one of the jugs with his elbow. Wine flooded the table. Everyone jumped up, shouting or laughing. At the same moment, a black bird soared through the door, heading straight for Jasmine.

'Kree!' Jasmine shouted, overjoyed.

Lief took advantage of the confusion to slip away. Only Sharn saw him go.

*

Lief let himself into the library and walked silently through the maze of shelves. His hand was on his sword. His mind was blank.

A dim light glowed in Josef's room. Lief paused and looked in. For a moment he thought he saw a hunched figure, ruler in hand, bent over something on the desk—something that Lief now knew must have been the plan of the chapel.

No . . . I have made no mistake. Oh, what wicked trickery is this? . . . If only I had remembered! Fool! Fool!

Then Lief blinked, and the vision was gone. The desk was empty, and Josef's body was lying on the bed. Tomorrow Josef would be laid to rest with all the ceremony befitting a Deltoran hero, but he would spend this night in his own, humble room.

'You will be avenged, Josef,' Lief said softly. 'Rest well.'

He glanced at the desk a second time as he turned to go. He had a niggling feeling that something about his fleeting vision had been wrong, but could not think what it could be.

He moved on to Paff's room. Here the curtains were open, and the room's air was golden with late afternoon light.

Paff lay propped up on pillows, exactly as Lief had seen her when he had first entered this room before sunrise. But she was no longer stiff and sweating. Her eyes were peacefully closed.

Beside her, in a chair dragged from behind the desk, sat Doom. A gleaming hunting knife lay across his knees. He raised his head as Lief entered the room. His shadowed face showed no surprise.

'Stay back, Lief,' he said softly.

'You know I cannot,' Lief said, moving forward.

Doom stared at him for a moment, then turned back to the sleeping girl. Her eyelids had begun to flutter.

'Soon she will wake,' he said. 'I should have cut her throat before this. I do not know why I hesitated.'

'Perhaps because you knew I would come,' Lief said. 'In your heart you know I must hear what she has to say.'

Doom shook his head restlessly. His long, brown fingers caressed the gleaming blade of the knife.

'You do not know what it is to be utterly alone, Lief,'

he said. 'You do not know the agony of having all you love torn from you. You have never felt the rage, the pain, the white-hot desire for revenge that burns from within until all that remains is dark despair, a yawning emptiness craving to be filled.'

'I have not felt it as you have,' Lief answered. 'But I have felt the evil force that promises to fill the emptiness with riches and power in return for service to its will. And I know that other choices can be made. You know it too, Doom.'

Doom shrugged, and half-smiled. The knife fell clattering to the floor.

Paff's eyes opened. She stared dreamily at the ceiling, then turned her head to look at Lief and Doom.

'Josef?' she murmured.

'Josef is dead,' Doom said in a level voice.

'So . . . he is silenced,' said the girl, her voice soft as a sigh. 'How he hated and feared you by the end, Doom. He feared you almost as much as I did. But—but it does not matter now, does it? Nothing matters now.'

Tears welled in her eyes. Slowly she relaxed her fingers, and the emeralds spilled onto the white bed cover.

'I tried so hard,' she whispered, her voice so faint that Lief had to bend to hear her. 'When I began, I had— such hopes! I thought of nothing but pleasing him. I did more—even more than he asked. And yet . . .'

'And yet at the last he turned his back on you,' Lief said. 'He abandoned you. Why, Paff? Why?'

The girl stared at him through her tears. 'Perhaps I tried too hard,' she whispered. 'Perhaps I did too much. My Master has many plans.'

And with the desperation of a trapped creature snatching at its only chance of escape, she threw herself forward and clutched the Belt of Deltora.

Lief tried to jump back, but Paff's grip was as strong as iron. He watched in horror as her face twisted, her back arched. There was a ghastly smell of burning. And with a cry that was more relief than pain, the failed, abandoned guardian of the south fell back on her pillows, released from her torment at last.

16 - Shocks

When Lief and Doom returned to the kitchen, they found it in uproar. Manus had joined the party at the table, but he was not the cause of the excitement and distress. The cause was Kree.

After hearing the news that four Kin were on their way bearing the gems Lief had asked for, Jasmine had discovered that the old injury on Kree's neck had re-opened. Trying to clean the freshly-flowing blood away, she had found something lodged inside the wound.

'It must have been buried deep, and gradually worked its way upward,' she said. 'No wonder the wound would not heal properly.'

She held the object out in the palm of her hand. It was a small grey glass bead. Red lines swirled within it.

Shuddering, Lief picked up the bead and threw it into the stove. It hissed, glowed briefly, then cracked and melted away.

'So now it is clear how our enemies always knew where we were,' Barda said heavily. 'We were only safe when Kree was not with us. He was carrying the Shadow Lord's eye, all along.'

Kree squawked loudly and indignantly.

'Of course you did not know, Kree,' Jasmine soothed. 'The device must have been put into your neck when you were drugged that first time you came back to Del. Someone in the palace did it—someone . . .'

'It was Paff,' Lief said quietly.

'*Paff?*' exploded Barda.

'Paff was the guardian of the south,' Lief said. 'But she will trouble us no more. The beast she sent to destroy us could withstand the power of the Belt, but she could not.'

The startled faces around the kitchen table grew sombre as the story of Paff's death was told. Lief and Doom did not relish the telling. Both felt they had failed.

'I wanted to spare her the horror of awakening,' Doom said. 'She had become a monster of wickedness, yet still I—I felt I understood how she had come to take the wrong path. She had lost everything. She was loved by no-one. Her misery had made her easy prey for the Shadow Lord.'

The corner of his mouth twisted in the familiar, mocking smile. 'But Lief wanted her alive, to tell what she knew,' he added. 'For once, Lief was the ruthless one. But Paff outwitted him.'

'Not for the first time,' Lief said grimly. 'She

deceived me completely. The black slime attacked us in the chapel just after Gla-Thon came running to tell us that Paff had taken a turn for the worse. But still I did not understand. It was only when Jasmine spoke of trances, and I remembered how Paff had looked in her room just before the dawn attack, that I realised what she was.'

'It was when I carried her out of the palace that I guessed it,' said Doom. 'She was as rigid as a stone statue. None of the other plague victims had been so.'

'I confess, I tried desperately to believe it was not true,' Lief muttered. 'I could not bear the thought that I had left Josef helpless in Paff's hands, to be kept drugged and confused, pumped for information and finally poisoned when she had no further use for him.'

'You are not the only one who will carry that burden till death,' muttered Ranesh.

'I am most at fault,' Doom said. 'Plainly Paff was poisoning Josef's mind against me for months. My impatience only made him fear and distrust me the more.'

'And you were reading his letters before they were sent,' Barda put in. 'No doubt he suspected you were changing them, or not sending them at all.'

'I think they *were* changed—at least one of them,' Lief said quietly.

He pulled out the letter he had received from Josef on their way to the Isle of the Dead.

'See here?' he said, tapping the two small pages.

Josef says he knows where we are going, but he fails to warn us of the danger lurking on Blood Lily Island. I could not understand that, but now I think I do.'

He held the pages out to Doom. 'Am I right in thinking that *Paff* delivered this to you for sending?' he asked.

'Indeed she did,' Doom frowned. 'Josef took an age to write his note, and I was impatient. I shouted from the entrance hall, and a few moments later Paff came running like a scared rabbit. I scanned the note on my way to the bird room. It was confused and scrappy enough, but I certainly did not change it.'

'No, but Paff did, on her way to you, I am sure of it,' Lief said. 'I think Josef scribbled on *three* pages of his little notebook. The second page contained the warnings that might have spared us much grief. Paff destroyed it, and tore off the right hand corners of the remaining pages, removing the page numbers, so we would not suspect.'

'Ah, she was cunning,' muttered Doom.

'Why, you almost sound as if you admire her!' growled Barda.

Doom grimaced. 'If she had chosen to use her talents for good, she might have been a great asset to us,' he said. 'Lief and I found supplies of that yellow paper beneath her mattress, you know. She never stopped thinking and planning. I am sure that by the end she had convinced Josef that I was working secretly for the Enemy.'

147

'I considered that myself, Doom,' Jasmine said calmly.

'Indeed?' Doom said, raising an eyebrow. 'And why was that?'

'Lief said the guardian of the south was subtle, quick-thinking, and very clever,' Jasmine answered, shrugging. 'That sounded more like you than anyone else in the palace.'

'Why, thank you,' Doom said drily.

'Also . . .' Jasmine checked the points off on her fingers. 'You have been in the Shadowlands. You are proud and ruthless. You mix with strange people. You are awake all hours of the night. You were one of the few to see Sharn the night she fell ill—'

'Why, plainly Paff went to my room that first night and put poison in my lip balm while I was still downstairs!' exclaimed Sharn, very shocked. 'Doom was the one who realised the cream was poisoned, when he brought the royal emeralds and amethysts to my chamber. He was the one who saved me!'

'And me,' Zeean put in. 'Jasmine, how *could* you think such a thing of your father?'

Jasmine shrugged again. 'Doom is not an ordinary father,' she said.

'Very true,' said Doom. 'And you are no ordinary daughter, I am happy to say. If I had been in your place, I would have thought exactly as you did. We are more alike than we realised, it seems.'

He grinned broadly, and Jasmine's tired face broke

into an answering smile.

Zeean and Sharn both shook their heads, clearly bewildered by this strange example of family loyalty.

Gers slammed his fist upon the table. 'Why do we sit here jabbering when there is a feast to be had?' he shouted. 'We are all here now, and my belly is growling!'

Ranesh grinned, and swung a large cloth bundle onto the table.

'Hardly a feast,' Marilen said, as the cloth was untied to reveal packets, jars and nets of glowing fruit. 'More a taste of what is to come. I could only bring what I could carry.'

As Gers, Gla-Thon and Lindal began tearing open the nets and packets, Barda grinned at Lief and Doom's startled faces. 'A trading ship has come, it seems,' he said.

'Just the first of many, the sailors said,' Marilen said happily. 'They said that the Bone Point Light has been noticed by all who sail the sea to our west, which they call the silver sea. Soon there will be food in plenty— enough, I am sure, to see the whole land through the winter.'

'Marilen was already on her way here when I left to fetch her,' Ranesh said, meeting Lief's eyes. 'We met not far from Del. She had been missing me, it seems.'

He spoke lightly, but Lief's heart warmed for him.

All is well, Lief told himself, as with shouts of delight everyone around him fell upon the delicious fruits, cheeses, dried fish, flat bread and little spiced cakes heaped upon the table. My feelings of foreboding were caused by exhaustion and fear, nothing more.

But still he could not relax. His nerves were tight as bow strings.

'Father tried to persuade me to change my mind, but I knew my place was here,' Marilen was chattering on. 'So I put on a garment that Sharn had left in Tora, picked up what food I could carry, and came.'

'If only you were Lindal's size,' bellowed Gers, with his mouth full. 'You could have carried five times as much!'

Everyone laughed. Ebony and Kree looked up from the shred of fish they were sharing and screeched. Even Filli, happily nibbling fruit peel, added his tiny voice to the general din.

All is well, Lief repeated to himself fiercely. It is over.

But he knew it was not. And as he bent his head unwillingly, he saw that the Belt knew it, too. The topaz was still shining like a golden star. But the ruby and the emerald were as pale and dull as roadside stones.

There was another burst of laughter around the table. Dazedly, Lief raised his head. He saw that Barda was ruefully displaying his wooden puzzle box, still locked despite the little rods sticking out from three of its carved sides.

'Plainly there is another lock on the fourth side!' cried Manus, holding out his hand. 'The trick is in the carving. Let me try it.'

'No, let me!' shrieked Zerry. 'Bess of the Masked Ones had many such puzzles. I could do it!'

'Oh, no,' growled Barda. 'This box will open for me, or not at all!'

Disdainfully he poked the box with his finger. His jaw dropped as with a tiny click, the fourth rod slid outward.

The lid of the box burst open. Out shot a laughing clown face, bouncing on a spring.

Barda yelled and dropped the box. Everyone shrieked in shock, then began to laugh helplessly.

The jack-in-the-box lay on its side on the table, its grinning head nodding foolishly, its tinny clockwork laughter running down.

Lief's skin crawled.

'Why, I spent hours on that foolish thing!' cried Barda in disgust. 'And for what? To have the life scared out of me.'

He tried to stuff the clown back into the box, but it would not go, and neither would the rods slide back in place. Clearly this was a puzzle that could be done one time only.

'Barda! Throw it in the fire!' Lief heard himself shouting harshly. His heart was beating like a drum.

'With pleasure,' Barda snorted, and tossed the box into the stove. It caught and burned merrily, quickly collapsing into ash.

What is *wrong* with me? Lief thought desperately. Why would a harmless toy terrify me so?

'Oh, that was a fine trick indeed!' gasped Manus, tears of mirth streaming down his cheeks. 'The rods hold the lid in place, with the clown pressed down beneath it. One rod removed—nothing. Two rods, three rods removed—still nothing. But when the last rod is removed—bang! Ah, Barda, if you had seen your face!'

He collapsed in fresh gales of laughter, echoed by the whole company.

Lief felt as if he was suffocating. He stood up abruptly and went outside. He sat down on the bench beside the back door and took a few deep breaths of cold fresh air.

The door opened again and Ranesh came out.

'I understand how you feel, Lief,' Ranesh said soberly. 'After all that has happened, it seems callous to be merry. But Josef would have rejoiced to hear us laugh.'

Lief's mind was filled once again with the memory of the frail old man bent over his desk, muttering as he studied the plan of the chapel. And again he had the feeling that something about the memory was wrong, or that there was something about it he did not understand.

Why do I keep fretting over this? he asked himself angrily. What more is there to understand? Josef guessed that the Sister of the South was beneath the chapel. He was horrified, and tried to contact me, to tell me. The night he died, he was studying the plan of the chapel to make absolutely sure—

And suddenly Lief's stomach seemed to turn over

152

as he realised that what he had just thought simply could not be true.

Josef could not have been studying the chapel plan the night he died, because the very next day, the plan was in its proper place, in a heavy box high in the storeroom.

Josef could not possibly have replaced the plan in that box. He could hardly walk, let alone stretch up to a high shelf. And if he had asked Paff to return the chapel plan for him, she would certainly have destroyed it.

But if Josef had not been studying the plan, what *had* he been doing?

17 - The Trap

Lief's mind was in turmoil. Why had he not remembered Josef's frailty? Why had he not realised that the old librarian must have been studying something that was already in his room?

Ranesh cleared his throat. Looking up, Lief realised that Ranesh was staring at him, holding out a stack of paper tied with pale blue ribbon.

'It is the manuscript of Josef's book,' Ranesh was saying. 'Josef wanted you to have it. I took it from his desk earlier, and it seemed right to give it to you now.'

Lief took the manuscript and, to please Ranesh, untied it. He lifted the top page, bearing the book's title, and looked at the next.

It was not a contents page or an introduction, as he had expected. It was a tale copied from the *Deltora Annals*, and when he saw which one, he felt cold to his very bones.

The Four Sisters

A Tenna Birdsong Tale from the Deltora Annals

Long ago, on a beautiful island set in a silver sea, there lived four sisters whose voices were as sweet as their hearts were pure. Their names were Flora, Viva, Aqua and Terra, and they had lived on the island so long that they had forgotten the number of the years.

The sisters loved to sing together, and their voices flowed over the island like soft, warm breeze by night and by day. Now and then a ship passed by, but to most of the sailors the sisters' song was like whispering leaves, lapping water, drifting sand, and the soft, secret rustling of small animals in the grass. The few who claimed to hear sweet voices were mocked by their fellows. But they knew what they had heard, and never forgot it until their dying days.

It so happened that a sorcerer came to that island, searching for a place to call his own. He heard the singing and hated it, as he hated all things good and beautiful, for although he was still young in years, he was old in wickedness.

He seized the four sisters and imprisoned each on a separate corner of the island. But the sisters still sang to one another from afar, and their song continued to bathe the island in peace and beauty by night and by day.

Maddened with rage, the sorcerer drew his cloak of shadows around him, and took up his magic staff. He stormed to each of the island's corners in turn and struck the sisters down, one by one.

First Flora's voice ceased. Then Viva's. Then Aqua's. For a time Terra sang on alone. But when her voice, too, was stopped, the island was silent.

And only then did the sorcerer realise what he had done. For in the very centre of the island, hidden deep within the earth, was a vile and hideous beast. Soothed by the singing of the four sisters, the beast had slept for centuries.

Now it awoke, in all its fury.

It rose, roaring, from its bed beneath the earth. It tore down the trees, crushed the small beasts, fouled the spring and smashed the mountains. It cracked the very rock on which the island rested, and the island began to sink.

In terror the sorcerer leaped into the silver sea. He conjured up a boat with a grey sail marked with red, and sailed away into the east, to find new lands to conquer.

The waves closed over the island and it has never been seen by human eye from that day to this. A few of the sailors who pass that way still claim to hear sweet voices singing beneath the water. They are mocked by their fellows, who hear only the sound of wind and waves. But the few know what they heard, and they never forget it, until their dying days.

Lief put down the second page with a shaking hand.

The Four Sisters . . . You . . . the sorcerer . . . you must stop . . .

Josef's halting words were echoing in his mind. And now they had a new and terrible meaning.

'It is too sad a tale to begin the book, I think,' said Ranesh, who had been reading over Lief's shoulder.

'Josef wrote it last,' Lief whispered, fighting the rising terror that was threatening to overwhelm him. 'He copied it out of the *Annals* and put it at the front of his manuscript, so I would be sure to see it at once if anything happened to him. He sent me a note—'

I must see you. Urgent. Fearful news . . .

Lief swallowed. 'The volume of the *Annals* was still lying open on his desk when I arrived. The tale was there, in its original form. But I did not read it.'

You are the sorcerer. You must stop . . .

Ranesh frowned in confusion. 'It is only an old folk tale. And surely Josef had told it to you before?'

If only I had remembered! Fool! Fool!

'His memory of it was hazy,' Lief said. 'He had forgotten the end. By the time he read it again, for his book, and realised what it might mean, I was far away.'

'"What it might mean"?' Ranesh exclaimed. 'I do not understand you!'

Was Josef writing out this tale when Doom came into his room last night? Lief thought. No. The *Annals* volume was far to his right—too far away for him to see it clearly. The manuscript was on his left, already neatly tied. And Josef was using a ruler. There are no ruled lines upon these pages.

So Josef must have been working on something else—something that was proof of what the tale had made him suspect.

After Doom left him, Josef must have hidden the proof somewhere close by, Lief thought. But surely he would have tried to tell me, or Ranesh, where it—

His heart jolted.

'Ranesh,' he said slowly. 'When Josef told you he wanted to be buried in his librarian's tunic, what exactly did he say?'

Ranesh stared. 'I told you—he could hardly speak. He just said, "In my tunic". He repeated it several times, very urgently, as if he thought I did not understand. But of course I knew exactly what he meant. Joseph had always said he wanted to be buried in the uniform of his office when the time came.'

'Was there anything in the tunic pocket?' Lief asked. He had begun to shiver all over.

Ranesh went very still. 'I did not look,' he said.

Plot . . . Treachery . . .

Lief stood up unsteadily, and staggered. Ranesh exclaimed in alarm, and took his arm.

As Ranesh half-carried Lief back into the kitchen, and lowered him into a chair, the talk and laughter around the table abruptly stopped. Jasmine, Barda and Doom leaped up. Sharn tried to rise.

'Look after him,' Ranesh said, and left the room.

Lief was already fumbling in his jacket pocket for the four fragments of the Four Sisters map. Suddenly he was sure he knew what Ranesh would find in Josef's tunic, and he could not wait.

He thrust the Four Sisters tale into Barda's hands. 'We have been tricked,' he muttered. 'The Enemy took more than the Sisters' names from this tale. He took the idea, and twisted it to fit his own purpose. If the *Deltora Annals* had been burned as he ordered—if Josef had not saved them—no-one would ever have known.'

He pulled the map fragments from his pocket and with trembling hands put them on the table in front of him. 'But Josef read it—realised the danger—tried to tell me. Perhaps, at the end, even Paff suspected it.'

My master has many plans . . .

As Barda, Jasmine and Doom began to read, Lief pushed the edges of the map fragments together. He took one look at the result, and his face began to burn.

. . . evil . . . the centre . . . the heart . . . the city . . . of . . .

'Doom, give me your knife,' he whispered, feeling for the blunt pencil that he had carried for so long.

Doom looked up from his reading, grim-faced. Without a word, he pulled the huge knife from its sheath, and put it on the table.

North . . . to south, east . . . to west . . . lines . . . map . . .

Lief placed the straight edge of the knife across the map and using it as a ruler, drew a line between Dragon's Nest and the Isle of the Dead. Then he moved the knife and ruled another line between Shadowgate and Del.

159

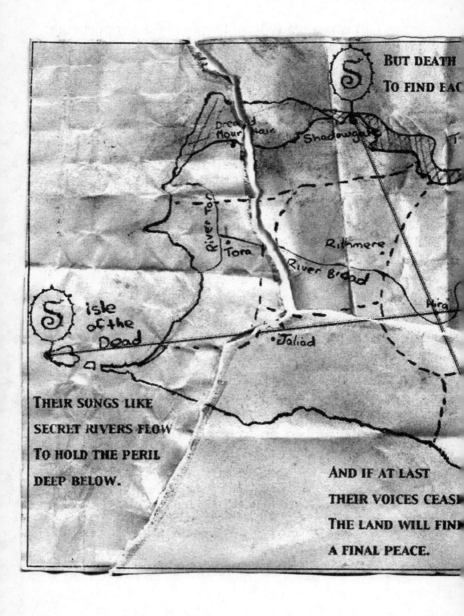

BUT DEATH

TO FIND EAC

Dread
Mountains

Shadowgate

River To

Tom

Rithmere

River Broad

Isle
of the
Dead

Hira

Jaliad

THEIR SONGS LIKE
SECRET RIVERS FLOW
TO HOLD THE PERIL
DEEP BELOW.

AND IF AT LAST
THEIR VOICES CEASE
THE LAND WILL FIN
A FINAL PEACE.

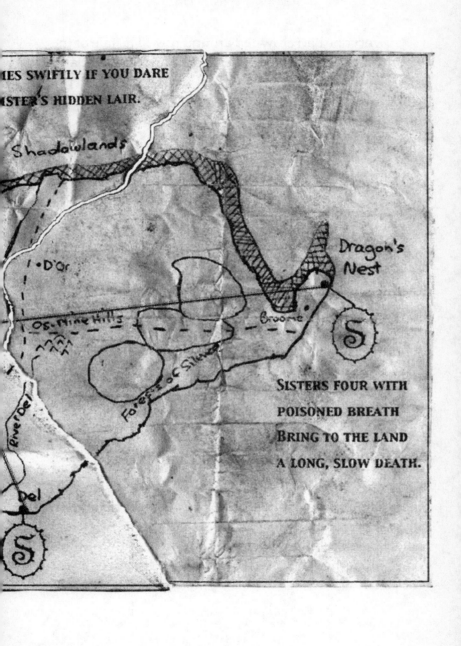

...IES SWIFTLY IF YOU DARE

...STER'S HIDDEN LAIR.

Shadowlands

D'Or

Os-Mine Hills

Dragon's Nest

Broome

Forests of Silence

River Del

Del

SISTERS FOUR WITH
POISONED BREATH
BRING TO THE LAND
A LONG, SLOW DEATH.

Everyone had crowded around now. The tale of the Four Sisters was being passed from hand to hand, and all those who had finished it were staring at the completed map, and at the lines Lief had drawn—the lines that crossed at the place marked 'Hira'.

Danger . . . Fearful . . . Here . . .

'Josef did not say "here", but "Hira",' Lief breathed aloud. 'The danger he was trying to warn me of was not the Sister of the South at all. It was an even greater peril, hidden in the centre of Deltora. In the City of the Rats.'

'I have always wondered why the people were driven out of the City,' Doom muttered. 'The Shadow Lord could have enslaved them where they were, if he had wished. But now I see. He wanted the City for his own purpose.'

'It was the *place* he wanted,' Lief said. 'The place where the Sister song lines would cross.'

Ranesh ran into the room, a paper in his hand. His face looked bleached. His eyes were wild.

'There *was* something in Josef's tunic!' he panted. 'It—'

Then he saw the map fragments lying on the table and put his paper down beside them. As Lief had expected, it was a copy of Doran's Dragon Territories map. The positions of all the Sisters had been marked, in Josef's handwriting. And between them Josef had ruled the same lines that Lief had just drawn—lines crossing in the territory of the opal, at Hira, the City of the Rats.

Lief pressed his hands together, trying to stop his hands from trembling.

'This was what Josef wanted me to see,' he said. 'He summoned me so urgently not to help me destroy the last Sister as I thought, and as Paff thought, too, but to *stop* me. He knew that if the voice of the last Sister was silenced, a terror worse than hunger would be unleashed upon Deltora.'

'So now we know why the Sister of the South was so easily destroyed,' Jasmine said quietly. 'With the other three Sisters gone, and the Bone Point Light restored, the Shadow Lord's game of starving us was all but over. He was impatient to spring his trap. He withdrew the last Sister's power, and abandoned Paff to fight on alone.'

His face set like stone, Barda read aloud the verse printed on the map.

Sisters four with poisoned breath
Bring to the land a long, slow death.
But death comes swiftly if you dare
To find each sister's hidden lair.
Their songs like secret rivers flow
To hold the peril deep below . . .
And if at last their voices cease
The land will find a final peace.

'"Final peace",' murmured Zeean. And suddenly the words, which had seemed so hopeful, were chilling.

'But Deltora is not a tiny island!' cried Gla-Thon, throwing down Josef's manuscript. 'No beast in the centre, however terrible, could destroy this whole land!'

'You are right, gnome,' growled Gers. 'Just let it try to invade the territory of the Jalis!'

'The Shadow Lord is not known for idle threats,' said Doom grimly. He swung around to Steven, who had remained silent ever since he saw the map.

'We must go at once to the City of the Rats,' he said. 'The bees and Mellow would be our fastest way. Will you—?'

Steven nodded shortly. His fists were clenched. His golden eyes were flickering brown. 'Our mother's orchard lies at the edge of the Plain of the Rats,' he said in a low voice. 'Mellow will fly like the wind to defend it.'

I will be faster, king of Deltora. And a full moon is rising.

The voice of the topaz dragon filled Lief's mind. The topaz grew hot beneath his hands. He felt Barda and Jasmine, close beside him. He turned to Doom.

'You go with Steven,' he murmured. 'Take as many from here as are able, with every weapon you can carry. We will meet you there.'

18 - The Revenge

The dragon flew faster than the wind, its golden scales glittering in the light of the huge, rising moon. The land slipped by beneath it. The first small lights were showing in villages and towns where people sat by their firesides, bathed their children or prepared their frugal meals, in ignorance of what was happening beyond the safety of their walls.

Flattened against the dragon's neck, Lief, Barda and Jasmine thought of nothing but holding on. The cold became more intense as they moved inland. The freezing wind buffeted them mercilessly.

We are crossing the border into opal territory. I have broken my vow.

The voice of the dragon hissed in Lief's mind. Defiance and regret were mingled in it, but there was no trace of fear.

If the opal dragon rises, I will explain, Lief replied.

The dragon snorted in grim amusement.

The land below them was flatter now, and more desolate. There were no more villages, no more towns. In the distance, water gleamed.

The bend of Broad River, Lief thought. We are nearly there.

His teeth had begun chattering again. The hair rose on the back of his neck as slowly he became aware of a sound rising beneath the rushing of the wind—a deep, ominous rumbling.

The next moment Jasmine screamed, and the dragon's scaly hide twitched beneath Lief's hands.

'What do you see?' Lief shouted. 'Jasmine—?'

And then he saw for himself, and the breath caught in his throat.

Beyond the gleam of the water, something huge was rising—a vast, rounded thing like a hideous reflection of the golden moon.

'By the heavens, what is it?' Barda shouted hoarsely.

The dragon growled, deep in its throat. It flew faster, faster. Now the sweeping bend of the river was directly ahead of them. And they could see, enclosed within the bend, the gigantic, poisonous yellow bubble pushing upward through the ruins of the City of the Rats, pushing the damaged buildings aside as if they were children's building bricks. A few rats were scattering from the ruins, squeaking shrilly as they ran.

Lief stared in terrified fascination as the bubble swelled and grew.

Their songs like secret rivers flow
To hold the peril deep below.

But the Sisters' song lines flowed through the earth no longer. And like the beast in the tale, like the clown in Barda's puzzle box, the Shadow Lord's revenge was rising from its long darkness, for now there was nothing to hold it down.

In a dream of horror Lief saw water beneath him. They were crossing the Broad. And the thing rising from the ruins of the City was still growing, swelling from the earth like a hideous boil.

How close do you wish to—?

The dragon's voice broke off as there was a thunderous roar from the other end of the plain. Something was hurtling towards them, rainbow colours flashing in the moonlight.

Instantly the dragon plunged earthward in a sickening dive. Lief, Barda and Jasmine shrieked as the ground came rushing up to meet them and they crashed to a stop. Dizzy and faint, their eyes streaming, they struggled to free themselves from the ropes that bound them.

'Make haste!' the dragon roared. It clawed at the ropes, cutting them through like threads.

The companions fell to the hard ground and rolled aside. The dragon spread its wings, preparing to take off once more.

'No!' shouted Lief. 'Do not fight! Be still! Stay on the ground!'

'And let that beast think I fear it? Never!' snarled the dragon, steam hissing from its terrible jaws.

'In Doran's name, I beg you!' Lief cried desperately.

The dragon growled. But it half-folded its wings and remained still.

The opal dragon was almost upon them. It was gigantic—even larger than the dragon of the emerald. The spines on its neck were fully raised. The beating of its wings was like thunder crashing, and the gale of its wingbeats hammered the ground.

The opal on the Belt was burning with rainbow fire. Lief pressed his fingers upon it, and sent his message with all the force of his being.

Dragon of the opal, do not attack! The topaz dragon is here at my wish.

He gasped as the opal dragon's blind, vengeful fury flashed through him like a lightning bolt. Summoning his strength, he tried again.

Dragon, you are blinded by your anger. A great evil is rising in your land—a far greater evil than a dragon who has crossed a border. Open your eyes and see it! In Dragonfriend's name, I beg you!

Again the name of Doran the Dragonlover worked its magic. Lief felt the rainbow dragon hesitate. He felt the battering of the wind on his back ease as the beast wheeled.

He crawled to his knees, looked ahead and groaned aloud.

The bubble had swelled even more. Its hideous bulk

now completely covered the ruined city, and rose as high as the palace in Del.

Lief stared at it in horrified fascination. At the bottom it was the same poisonous yellow as it had been before. But at the top it was paler—paler, tighter and shinier. As if . . . as if . . .

With a ghastly tearing sound the top of the bubble split open. A fountain of vile, dull grey liquid, thick as heavy cream, gushed up into the air.

Lief heard the dragons roar. He heard Barda and Jasmine crying out in revulsion beside him. And he heard something else, he was sure of it—the sound of distant, wicked laughter.

The spouting liquid began flowing to the ground, spreading outward in a thick grey flood.

'What is it?' Jasmine shrieked, her eyes wide with horror.

A red-eyed rat, more daring than the others, darted at the grey liquid, perhaps hoping it was something good to eat. The moment the liquid touched it, the rat stiffened and fell, its legs jerking convulsively.

The companions watched, horrified, as the grey liquid covered the rat's twitching body and flowed on, moving very fast. The remaining rats shrieked and ran away from it, scattering outward across the plain.

'It is poisonous,' hissed Barda.

'And it is alive,' Lief muttered. 'It is alive—and growing.'

He knew it was true. The thick, grey fluid was

making more of itself, and more, feeding on the earth and the air.

There was a blaze of fire as the opal dragon swooped, roaring at the spreading circle of grey. Multicoloured flame seared a great patch at the edge of the flood. The patch stiffened and hardened. The grey mass of liquid on either side of it closed in and flowed on, covering the burned place swiftly, as the rat had been covered.

The opal dragon wheeled and roared again. Again flame seared the moving ground, and again the burned place was smothered in an instant and the circle of grey grew larger.

'We should return to the air, king of Deltora,' the topaz dragon murmured, watching its rival's efforts placidly. 'The rainbow beast is well occupied. It will not trouble us. And the grey poison is spreading fast. This ground will not be safe for long.'

Plainly it was right. The companions scrambled back onto its neck, and in moments were gasping in the cold air, clinging for their lives as the dragon soared upward.

The beast flew a little way across the river, then turned in the air and hovered. 'It is fortunate we did not delay,' it commented.

Shivering, Lief, Barda and Jasmine looked down.

In the few minutes that had passed since the dragon took flight, the place where they had been standing had become a sea of grey. The whole of the land enclosed by the river bend was almost covered. Driven back to the river banks, hundreds of rats had begun leaping for the water, squealing in terror. Other rats were running for their lives across the plain to the north, just keeping ahead of a sweeping grey tide.

The opal dragon was wheeling over the grey sea, blasting it with rainbow fire. But the grey was still increasing, and every moment it seemed to be moving faster.

'Nothing will stop it,' Lief heard himself saying.

'The river will stop it,' Barda said firmly. 'The Plain of the Rats is bounded by water on all sides. And the plain itself is no loss. There is no drearier place in the whole of Deltora.'

'Very true,' said the topaz dragon, yawning widely. 'It is not territory worth saving.'

'Would you feel the same if it was yours?' Jasmine asked sharply.

The topaz dragon blinked.

The grey reached the river and began pouring over the banks into the water. And if anything the water seemed to strengthen it. The grey circle seemed to double in size almost instantly. The rippling water flattened and thickened. Squealing, swimming rats were overtaken and swallowed up.

Barda cursed in disbelief. Jasmine cried out.

The topaz dragon roared and arched its neck. Golden fire poured from its snarling jaws, searing the grey stream spilling over the river bank below.

But Lief was silent, looking back to the centre of the circle.

The collapsed yellow bubble was now hidden beneath a lumpy blanket of grey. The shapes of the ruins of the City of the Rats were visible around it—but only the shapes. Every ravaged building, every fallen tower, every brick and stone, was covered in a thick grey shroud.

And here the grey no longer moved, and no longer shone in the moonlight. It was setting hard.

Lief's nightmare vision slid back into his mind, and his blood ran cold.

Grey, barren land. The skeletons of trees. A grey river, sluggish water thick as mud, with huge grey fish lying dead on the wrinkled surface . . . Monstrous creatures shrieking in the sky . . .

Not the Shadowlands, but Deltora. He knew that now.

This was a monster they could not fight. The grey tide would continue to spread. It would swallow rivers, forests and plains. It would cover towns and villages and farms. It would fill the valleys and smooth out the hills.

Nothing in its path would be spared. Death would come equally to the ferocious Sand Beasts and to the gentle Kin, to the flesh-eating Grippers and to the wondrous Lilies of Life.

Some of the grey would age and set hard, turning rivers to sludge, encasing houses, beasts, crops, trees and people alike in a shell of stone. The rest would move on.

The people who could outrun it would be driven to the coast, to fight over boats or mill helplessly at the water's edge like the rats on the river bank. Or they would climb mountains and wait, freezing on the peaks, as the grey climbed, climbed . . .

And at last, Deltora, all its variety and strangeness lost forever, would be one great, cold, grey plain.

This was what the Shadow Lord's malice and desire for vengeance had decreed must be, if the king who had been foretold did arise, restore the Belt of Deltora and rid the land of tyranny.

I never have just one plan . . .

The Shadow Lord knew that this new king would certainly attempt to destroy the magic crystal which was Deltora's last link to the Shadowlands. He knew that, aided by the Belt, the king would be powerful enough to do it at last.

So the crystal was set to reveal the plot of the Four Sisters as it died. Then the king who had dared to defy the Shadow Lord would learn why his land was starving.

He would learn of the Four Sisters.

And, of course, he would set out to destroy them.

Lief gritted his teeth as one by one the pieces of the plan fell into place.

He had taken the bait offered to him without a second thought. The Enemy had set a trap for him, then dared him, forced him, to walk into it.

Looking back, Lief could hardly believe he had been so easily tricked.

Not once had he wondered why the map showing where the Sisters were had not been destroyed, but had been torn into four parts. Not once had he wondered why each fragment had been hidden with a Sister, to be easily found if that Sister and its guardian were destroyed.

Not once had he considered that the verse placed on the map might have a double meaning.

And not once had he wondered why the stone protecting the last Sister had not been a sober warning, but an insulting dare, almost guaranteed to make him take the last, fatal step.

But now, too late, he saw the reasons for all these things. And he saw that, from the beginning, the Shadow Lord had arranged things so that Deltora would be his, whatever happened.

Anger rose in him—a helpless, white-hot anger.

'It has been the Enemy's pleasure to make us choose unknowingly which way the land would die,' he muttered. 'If we failed in our quest, the land would die slowly. If we succeeded, death would come swiftly. Either way, the Shadow Lord would win.'

And as the last words left his lips, the first dead fish floated to the wrinkled surface of the dying river, and with weird, howling cries, the seven Ak-Baba came swooping in from the north.

19 - Dragon Night

Rage dissolving into numb horror, Lief saw the opal dragon swing to face the shrieking beasts hurtling over the horizon. He felt the muscles of the dragon of the topaz jerk violently beneath him. Then the dragon's neck twisted, and the terrible head turned. Lief was caught and held by the fathomless gaze of a flat, golden eye.

'The Enemy has sensed our attacks on the grey tide, no doubt,' the dragon hissed. 'He has sent his killing creatures to protect it. He must be using powerful sorcery indeed to defy the power of the Belt of Deltora.'

It glanced down at the seared section of river bank below, and snorted. 'There is little enough damage. But the Enemy fears dragons, it seems. Even two are too many for him. I must set you and your companions down, king of Deltora. When the pack has finished with the dragon of the opal, it will come for me.'

'No!' Lief exclaimed. 'There is still time for you to get away from here. Turn and—'

The golden eye flickered. 'I would rather die fighting than fleeing,' the dragon said. 'And I am sick of hiding.'

'As the grey tide spreads, there will be nowhere left to hide, in any case!' shouted Jasmine, as Kree screeched wildly, wheeling in the sky above her. 'You must keep us with you, dragon! The Belt will aid you— and we can fight!'

'Indeed we can,' growled Barda, drawing his sword.

'No!' Lief cried frantically again. 'Barda, Jasmine—'

He felt Jasmine's hand close on his, and saw the gleam of Barda's savage grin.

'We know full well that you will not leave the dragon now, Lief,' Jasmine shouted. 'And we will not leave you. We were together at the beginning of this, and so we will be at the end.'

'And if you will take a soldier's advice, dragon, you will not wait to be attacked,' roared Barda. 'You will go forward and fight beside your brother!'

'That opal beast is no brother of mine,' the dragon snarled.

'It is more your brother than the seven Ak-Baba!' Jasmine screamed furiously. 'Will you leave it to be torn apart, while you wait your turn?'

The dragon bared its terrible fangs. Its black tongue flickered. Then its eyes seemed to glow.

'Very well,' it growled. 'Together we will fight beside the dragon of the opal, and together we will die. This battle will be our last. But while we live, we will do the Enemy what damage we can, for the sake of our doomed land, and for our ancestors, and for our young, who now will never be.'

It flung itself forward, streaking over the sea of grey, towards the Ak-Baba.

And as Lief drew his sword and screwed his stinging eyes shut, he saw behind his lids words from *The Belt of Deltora*—words that had always filled him with dread and now had a new and terrible meaning for him.

. . . the Enemy is clever and sly . . . to its anger and envy a thousand years is like the blink of an eye . . .

The book called the Enemy 'it'. The unknown writer had understood something that Lief himself had never quite accepted until this moment.

However he had begun, the Shadow Lord was now far more—or perhaps far less—than a cruel tyrant who was a master of sorcery.

Long ago, perhaps, he had been a merely a sorcerer, with a cloak of shadows and a boat with a grey sail marked in red. He had felt fear, suffered a bitter defeat, and sailed east across a silver sea to find new lands to conquer.

But if he was human then, he was human no longer.

Envy, hatred and malice had consumed his humanity long ago, burned it away to dust. All that remained were memories.

'He' had become 'it'—a force for evil that fed on power, that destroyed and corrupted everything it touched. A force that would never die.

I have many plans . . . Plans within plans . . .

How did I ever think that I could defeat the Shadow Lord? Lief thought bitterly. For a thousand years he has worked towards his goal. And we—we have struggled in his web, blindly, stupidly, repeating the mistakes of our ancestors. In his time, Doran the Dragonlover was called mad. In our time, Josef was insulted and avoided. Over and over again we have ignored the lessons of history . . .

Learn the lessons of history . . . Despair is the enemy. Do not let it defeat you . . .

The roars of the dragons were like thunder. The blood-curdling shrieks of the seven Ak-Baba split the air. Jasmine and Barda were shouting. Kree was screeching. They were battered by wind thick with smoke and the bitter smell of burning hair, dust and rotting flesh that was the odour of the seven Ak-Baba.

But Lief had ceased to hear, to smell, to feel. His mind was turned inward and his skin was prickling. For as the memory of Zeean's faint, halting voice had faded away, another voice had taken its place.

. . . the Enemy fears dragons, it seems. Even two are too many for him . . .

178

The Shadow Lord had thought of everything. But he had not planned on dragons.

Lief opened his eyes. The Ak-Baba had almost reached them. He could see their eyes, like burning pools of madness. He could see their talons, flexed ready to rip and tear. He could see their beaks gaping, their needle-sharp teeth glinting.

He pressed his fingers to the amethyst. He called silently, but with all his strength.

Veritas!

And as he thought the name, more words followed it into his mind. He realised that he was remembering the strange, foreign words that had flowed into him from Doran's soul stone as he pressed it into the earth.

Veritas hopian forta fortuna fidelis honora joyeu . . .

And suddenly he knew what the words were. Not a sentence, but a list of names. The most important names in Doran's life.

He pressed his free hand to the Belt once more, running his fingers across every gem.

Veritas! Hopian! Forta! Fortuna! Fidelis! Honora! Joyeu! Come to our aid, I pray you! For Doran. For the land!

He felt the dragon of the topaz jerk beneath him, saw the dragon of the opal turn abruptly, its rainbow eyes blazing.

And then the seven Ak-Baba were upon them—the Ak-Baba were surrounding them, howling like savage wolves, snarling and snapping, claws and teeth ripping and tearing.

179

They worked as a pack, attacking from all sides, from above, from below. Three or four would distract their enemies by ferocious charges while the others moved in swiftly under the cover of their wings.

They were vicious, fearless, tireless. They bore the scars of countless battles and were filled with ancient cunning. But rarely had they faced two dragons at one time, and never had they faced a dragon aided by swords, and by the Belt of Deltora.

They screeched with rage as the dragons clawed at them and blasted them with fire. They howled as Lief, Barda and Jasmine slashed at them, preventing them from closing in. Diving at them from above, as fearless as they were, Kree drove his sharp beak into their necks, their heads, distracting and enraging them the more.

Then one fell—one fell, its throat torn open by a single slash of the opal dragon's talons. Screeching and twisting it plunged to earth, to be engulfed almost instantly by the grey tide.

The dragons roared in triumph. Lief, Barda and Jasmine cheered. But the remaining Ak-Baba charged, shrieking ferociously, and the opal dragon's roar became a bellow of agony as the soft underside of its neck was pierced by teeth like needles and claws like sharpened iron.

An Ak-Baba with a speckled head was clinging to the dragon's neck, clinging to it upside down, like a giant bat. Blood flowed from the sides of its gaping beak, dripped over its clawed feet. Howling at the smell of the blood, the other Ak-Baba closed in. In seconds the rainbow dragon was lurching in the air, its body almost hidden beneath a shrieking mass of twisting, snake-like necks and vast, flapping wings.

'Help it!' Jasmine screamed. 'Oh, make haste!'

'It is finished,' growled the dragon of the topaz. 'This is how they end it.'

'No!' roared Lief. 'Get below it!'

The dragon wheeled and soared beneath the struggling mass of bodies. Now the speckled Ak-Baba was directly above them, its ragged wings wrapped around the dragon's neck, its ghastly body flattened against the dragon's hide.

Lief and Barda hesitated, suddenly fearful that if they slashed with their swords they would fatally wound the dragon as well as the beast attacking it.

But Jasmine jumped upright, balancing on the topaz dragon's neck as lightly and easily as once she had surveyed the Forests of Silence from the branch of a storm-tossed tree. Her dagger flashed as she reached up and plunged it into the back of the Ak-Baba's neck, just below the head.

The vast bird stiffened. It made a hideous, gurgling sound.

'Go!' roared Barda.

Jasmine tore her dagger free. Lief caught her by the waist and held her fast, pulling her down as the topaz dragon sped away, and behind them the speckled Ak-Baba dropped like a stone.

There was no moment of triumph this time. Freed from its clinging tormentor, the opal dragon was twisting in the air, slashing and roaring fire at the other beasts tearing at its body. But its movements were clumsy. It was weakening.

And the topaz dragon was weakening too. Its enormous strength had been drained by the terrible struggle with the two-faced beast, drained further by the flight to the Plain of the Rats. All over its golden body, old wounds had begun oozing blood.

The Ak-Baba knew it. They could see the beast's uneven wingbeats. They could smell the blood.

Shrieking, they abandoned the floundering body of the dragon of the opal, and sped in for the kill. There were only five remaining, but those five were as fresh, as ferocious, as ravenous for blood as they had been at the beginning.

They flew, screeching, through the golden fire and hit the topaz dragon full in the side. It lurched, tilted, lost height, its huge wings beating desperately, its spiked tail lashing. The Ak-Baba pursued it, surrounded it, moved in again.

'This time, we are lost, I fear,' growled the topaz dragon thickly. 'But let us try to take another of them with us.'

And at that moment there was a roar from above them, and the sky seemed to explode in a burning mass of shooting stars. The Ak-Baba scattered, howling in shock. Lief, Barda and Jasmine cowered against the

182

dragon's scales, coughing in a haze of smoke that stank of singed hair and scorched cloth. And out of the heavens soared the dragon of the lapis-lazuli, wings spangled with stars, starry fire belching from its snarling jaws.

The Ak-Baba wheeled in the air, turning to face it, snake-like necks stretching, beaks gaping wide as they howled in fury. Then suddenly, one was gone, snatched out of the air. There was a sickening crack as its neck broke between vast red jaws.

And as its lifeless body was tossed aside, as the ruby dragon bellowed its triumph and the remaining Ak-Baba shrieked and howled defiance, a ball of emerald fire roared through the smoke haze.

Three of the shrieking beasts dived. The fourth was too slow. The fire ball struck. The feathers of its wings burst into flames and it plummeted to the ground, trailing a plume of fire.

Now only three Ak-Baba remained. Through the smoke and fire they could see five vast, glittering shapes, five snarling sets of fangs, five lashing tails. They shrieked defiantly, hovering, weighing the odds.

But when there was yet another roar, and a gush of purple flame lit the sky in the west, they twisted in the air and fled.

And the dragons did not follow. For by the light of the great, golden moon they could see the grey tide below. They could see it spreading before their eyes. They could feel its deadening chill. They knew what they must do.

20 - Full Circle

Speechless, Lief, Barda and Jasmine clung to the topaz dragon as it flew to take its place in the circle of dragons surrounding the grey sea. They watched in wonder as the dragons dropped lower, lower and hovered.

Then, without a word or signal, the dragons roared.

Flame gushed from their jaws. Flame of green, gold and scarlet. Flame of purple and silver-white. Blue flame filled with stars, and flame that burned with all the colours of the rainbow.

. . . the Enemy fears dragons, it seems. Even two are too many for him . . .

And what of six? Lief thought. Then he changed the number to seven, for he saw the baby diamond dragon gravely hovering beside Veritas, adding her own small, silver-white flame to the fire.

The edges of the grey tide scorched and blackened,

and when the circle was bounded by a broad black band, the dragons began moving slowly, patiently inward. Whenever they breathed, they breathed fire, and wherever the fire fell, the grey burned and died. And no dragon moved on while any patch of grey remained.

On and on the dragons moved, their circle tightening, as the great moon rose and paled and stars filled the blackness of the sky.

Gradually the grey inside the circle grew less, and the black band outside it grew broader. By the time Steven's caravan pulled to a halt on the bank of the clogged River Broad, the people who tumbled out to stare in wonder could see more black than grey.

And at last the dragons were so close together that the tips of their wings were touching. Together they roared, and the colours of their fires mingled in a rainbow blaze. And when that last, great fire had died, nothing remained of the Shadow Lord's terror but a vast circle of blackened ash.

In the centre of the dark circle the dragons hovered, as if unwilling to end the moment. Diamond, emerald, lapis-lazuli, topaz, opal, ruby and amethyst, they joined to relish their triumph, grieve for what had been lost, and look to the future.

And all who looked upon that scene were swept by a great wave of joy and wonder. For they saw that the shining wings of the dragons were like the gems of the Belt of Deltora, blazing in the sky.

And so it was that the last plan of the Shadow Lord was undone by the will of Deltora's last dragons, and the kingdom of Deltora was safe.

In years to come, the story would become a legend. The night called Dragon Night would be Deltora's greatest festival of the year, celebrated with feasts, dancing, games, and circles of fireworks from across the silver sea. Children dressed as Lief, Barda and Jasmine would ride dragons made of painted wood and shining cloth, and at midnight a great bonfire would be lit in every town and village in the land, and Deltora would ring with cheers.

But the people who witnessed that first Dragon Night from the other side of the River Broad were too awe-struck to cheer. As it happened, or perhaps because fate had decreed it, every one of Deltora's seven dragon territories was represented among them. For Steven had said that Zerry of the Mere must have his place in the caravan, and Zerry, his eyes dark with wonder, was standing with the rest, for once lost for words.

Lief himself could do no more than silently give thanks. But when at last the dragons settled to the earth, onto the blackened circle they had made, he felt their unblinking eyes upon him and knew he had to speak. And he knew what he had to say.

'My name is Lief,' he said, and bowed his head. 'Forgive me for using the names that Dragonfriend carried in his heart. I did it for the sake of our land, and his.'

The dragons considered. Then they all bowed in reply, even the emerald dragon of honour, if rather stiffly.

'It is not so easy, however,' it said. 'You called us all at the same time. Now we know each other's true names, as well as yours, for any fool could guess which dragon name is which. This is an evil that cannot be undone.'

Lief swallowed. 'It cannot be undone,' he said. 'But perhaps it is not an evil.'

The emerald dragon snorted. 'To know a being's true name is to give power over that being,' it said.

'Then we all have power over one another,' said the dragon of the lapis-lazuli pertly. 'And I, for one, have no intention of risking your revenge—Honora.'

The emerald dragon bared its teeth. 'Very wise— Fortuna,' it hissed, but said no more.

'What is my name?' squeaked the little diamond dragon.

'Your name is Forta,' said Veritas. 'Forta—after your mother.'

✳

At dawn, three dragons flew into Del—golden Fidelis, scarlet Joyeu, and Fortuna, the dragon of the lapis-lazuli.

Fidelis carried Lief, Barda and Jasmine. Joyeu carried Doom, Lindal and Manus. Fortuna carried Gla-Thon, Ranesh and Gers. Gers, his broad face pale as paper, was seen to kiss the ground when the ride was over, but swore till his dying day that he had merely stumbled.

Though it was so early, and though few in Del had

any idea of the peril their land had just escaped, the city was alive with rejoicing people. Most had been awake all night.

First, four Kin had arrived from Dread Mountain, their pouches bulging with gems to heal the sick and test the remaining food. Then the city gates had flown open of themselves, and Torans by the hundred had swept in, drawing carts piled high with food from across the silver sea.

Some yellow notices still blew, trampled and muddy, on the streets. But no-one noticed them or cared.

The dragons crouched uneasily together on the palace lawn as their passengers slid from their backs. They accepted renewed thanks gravely, then prepared to depart, for Joyeu and Fortuna felt like trespassers, and Fidelis longed for the hills.

'I hope I may see you again, king of Deltora,' Fidelis said. 'But I will not come again to Del. The spears and arrows of your friends are not pleasing to me.'

Gla-Thon winced, but Lindal lifted her chin.

'I regret harming you, dragon,' she said loudly and clearly. 'But I believed you were destroying the palace, as once the red dragons destroyed ancient Capra, out of envy for its beauty.'

'Indeed?' Fortuna said with interest.

The dragon of the ruby hissed. Its red eyes darkened.

'You have been listening to lies, I fear, woman of Broome,' it said stiffly, after a moment's tense silence.

'My ancestors destroyed Capra, certainly. But why would dragons envy a small, pink city made of stones? The whole of the east was the ruby dragons' kingdom— a kingdom of land, sea and sky far more beautiful than a city could ever be.'

Lief's throat tightened. He saw at once that the dragon was right.

Lindal stared in confusion.

'The Capricons were most proud of the city they had built,' the dragon went on softly. 'They planted elegant trees all around it, trees hung with hundreds of little red lanterns. Did you know that, woman of Broome?'

'I have heard of it,' Lindal said warily, plainly wondering where this was leading.

'And did you know,' the dragon asked, even more softly, 'that those pretty lanterns were made of dragons' eggs? Live eggs, stolen from nests while the dragons were away fishing? Eggs sucked dry, then fitted with candles and strung on the trees to make the city beautiful?'

Lindal seemed to freeze where she stood. Lief felt the blood drain from his face. He wanted to bow his head in shame, but he could not look away from the dragon's darkened eyes.

'Three times did the ruby dragons warn that the slaughter of their young must stop,' the dragon said. 'But the Capricons were proud, and drunk with their desire to add to Capra's splendour. The plunder increased. And so, at last, the dragons stopped it, in their own way.'

Lindal wet her lips. 'I see now how it was,' she said. 'I heard only one side of the story, and this led me to judge your tribe unfairly. I beg your pardon.'

The dragon stared at her, unblinking. 'I accept your apology,' it said at last. 'And though I refuse to swear an oath that is an insult to my ancestors, I make this promise to you, as friend to friend. I will not harm any human in my land, as long as no human in my land harms me or my kin.'

'Thank you,' Lindal said humbly. 'I can ask no more. And I will tell them. I will tell them all.'

One bright morning the following spring, when Deltora was filled with blossom, when bees were drunk with nectar and birds filled the air with song, Jasmine put on a green silk dress, threaded flowers in her hair, and went out to meet Lief on the palace hill.

Hand in hand they were married there, before a crowd the like of which Del had never seen. Barda stood beside Lief. Marilen stood beside Jasmine. Sharn and Doom looked on, and remembered.

Lindal was watching, with a laughing, dancing crowd from Broome. Gla-Thon was there from Dread Mountain, with old Fa-Glin, Pi-Ban who had shared the companions' adventure in the Shadowlands, and the gentle Kin, Ailsa, Bruna, Merin and Prin.

There were Torans in their hundreds, Zeean at their

head, silken robes fluttering like butterflies.

Manus and the people of Raladin were present, their flutes filling the air with gladness. Fardeep the hermit, now once again master of the Games Inn of Rithmere, clapped his hands and sang with Orwen and Joanna, games champions of the Mere. Gers and a troop of Jalis stood proudly with Hellena, Claw and Brianne, Resistance fighters of the Shadowlands.

All the men and women of the old Resistance were present. All the freed prisoners from the Shadowlands were there. And Zerry, magician's apprentice of the Masked Ones, now chief assistant to the new palace stable master, and wearing his first new suit of clothes for the celebration, made sure that Honey, Bella and Swift saw everything that passed.

Every friend the companions had made on their travels was present to wish them well, from Tira of Noradz to Steven and Queen Bee of the Plains, from Bede and Mariette of Shadowgate to Nanion and Ethena of D'Or.

Even Tom the shopkeeper had taken a holiday in honour of the great event, and appeared in dusty finery with his sister Ava on his arm.

And the dragons Veritas, Forta, Hopian, Honora, Fortuna, Fidelis and Joyeu circled in the sky above.

But for Lief and Jasmine it was as if they were quite alone, for both of them were gaining the dearest wish of their hearts.

In days to come, while the infant Josef slept in a

basket beside her, Marilen would write the story of their marriage in the *Deltora Annals*, for she was the palace librarian now. Ranesh had more than enough to do, for Doom had left for parts unknown. Doom wanted to stretch his legs and his mind, he said, and to find out if it was true that a dragon can lay eggs without a mate, if the need arises. He would meet them in Broome in the summer, when Barda and Lindal wed. He knew the celebrations of Broome, he said, and would not miss this one for the world.

And so life went on in Deltora, and life was good.

Barda and Lindal had six children, all of them taller than their parents, and as alike as peas in a pod.

Lief and Jasmine had a daughter, Anna, and twin boys, Jarred and Endon.

And sometimes Doom, home from one of his many journeys and silently watching the twins at play, would remember two other boys running through the palace gardens, long ago. And he would smile.

With Jasmine by his side, Lief ruled the land long and wisely. But he never forgot that he was a man of the people, and that their trust in him was the source of his power. Neither did he forget that the Enemy, though defeated, was not destroyed. He knew that the Enemy was clever and sly, and that to its anger and envy a thousand years was like the blink of an eye. So he wore the Belt of Deltora always, and never let it out of his sight.